*Here's what reviewers
are saying about*
TO HAVE AND TO HOLD

"At last a line that goes beyond the 'happily ever after' ending.... What really makes these books special is their view of marriage as an exciting, vibrant blossoming of love out of the courtship stage. Clichés such as the 'other woman' are avoided, as family backgrounds are beautifully interwoven with plot to create a very special romantic glow."
—Melinda Helfer, *Romantic Times*

"At last, a series of honest, convincing and delightfully reassuring stories about the joys of matrimonial love. Men and women who sometimes doubt that a happy marriage can be achieved should read these books."
—Vivien Jennings, *Boy Meets Girl*

"I am extremely impressed by the high quality of writing within this new line. Romance readers who have been screaming for stories of romance, sensuality, deep commitment and love will not want to miss this line. I feel that this line will become not only a favorite of mine but of the millions of romance readers."
—Terri Busch, *Heart Line*

*"Jenny," Mister said,
wrapping her securely in his arms.
"They're all gone.
We can start the kissing now."*

"What? And make more babies?"

As his soft, heated lips fell onto his wife's, he murmured, "Someone ought to have a talk with *you*. Preferably Amy. *She* knows kissing doesn't give you babies."

Jenny felt the powerful encouragement of Mister's tender lips. She fell under their spell the way she always did, sinking deeper and deeper into the enchantment with each excruciatingly soft touch of his moist, full mouth on hers...

Dear Reader:

Last month we were delighted to announce the arrival of TO HAVE AND TO HOLD, the thrilling new romance series that takes you into the world of married love. This month we're pleased to report that letters of praise and enthusiasm are pouring in daily. TO HAVE AND TO HOLD is clearly off to a great start!

TO HAVE AND TO HOLD is the first and only series that portrays the joys and heartaches of marriage. Its unique concept makes it significantly different from the other lines now available to you, and it offers stories that meet the high standards set by SECOND CHANCE AT LOVE. TO HAVE AND TO HOLD offers all the compelling romance, exciting sensuality, and heartwarming entertainment you expect.

We think you'll love TO HAVE AND TO HOLD—and that you'll become the kind of loyal reader who is making SECOND CHANCE AT LOVE an ever-increasing success. Read about love affairs that last a lifetime. Look for three TO HAVE AND TO HOLD romances each and every month, as well as six SECOND CHANCE AT LOVE romances each month. We hope you'll read and enjoy them all. And please keep writing! Your thoughts about our books are very important to us.

Warm wishes,

Ellen Edwards

Ellen Edwards
TO HAVE AND TO HOLD
The Berkley Publishing Group
200 Madison Avenue
New York, N.Y. 10016

To Have and to Hold

THE FAMILY PLAN
NURIA WOOD

SECOND CHANCE AT LOVE
BOOK

*For my loving husband, Victor,
with infinite thanks*

THE FAMILY PLAN

Copyright © 1983 by Nuria Wood

Distributed by The Berkley Publishing Group

All rights reserved. No part of this publication may be reproduced or transmitted in any form or by any means, electronic or mechanical, including photocopy, recording, or any information storage and retrieval system, without permission in writing from the publisher.

Requests for permission to make copies of any part of the work should be mailed to: Permissions, To Have and to Hold, The Berkley Publishing Group, 200 Madison Avenue, New York, NY 10016.

First edition published November 1983

First printing

"Second Chance at Love," the butterfly emblem, and "To Have and to Hold" are trademarks belonging to Jove Publications, Inc.

Printed in the United States of America

To Have and to Hold books are published by
The Berkley Publishing Group
200 Madison Avenue, New York, NY 10016

1

"WAITING FOR SOMEONE?" the man's silky voice breathed into her ear.

Jenny hesitated for a split second too long. "No?" she said tentatively.

When she stole a glance at him, the man's dark eyes were laughing. "Well, are you or aren't you?" he asked, leaning over the bar to get the bartender's attention. He indicated that Jenny's glass be refilled.

"No, no, please," she cut in, touching the stranger's back. She instantly drew her hand away, as though from a hot baking dish. How typical of her to think in household similes, she reprimanded herself.

By now she was sure that the color of her face matched her low-cut red silk blouse and spindly high-heeled shoes. She had the distinct impression that she should take charge here, and taking charge was one of the things she did best— under normal circumstances. She patted the stool next to hers. "Sit down," she directed the man.

"I like standing close to you," he intoned as he slid her

second glass of seltzer water toward her.

What had she gotten herself into in just ten minutes of being alone in this place? "Just sit!" she ordered. She winced at the way she sounded—like a mother commandeering a brood of children.

With relief she watched the man retreat a step and lean into the leather barstool. He must be married, Jenny thought with an ironic smile. Someone had him well trained. No sooner had the thought crossed her mind than she regretted it. She was trying to *change* her old ways of thinking. Darn. This was going all wrong.

The man leaned close to Jenny and cupped her cheek as he whispered into her ear, "My name's Hendrick."

"Hendrick?" she repeated, flustered. She'd never come across that name in one of her what-to-name-baby books.

He nodded, seemingly pleased with himself.

Jenny carefully removed his hand, patting it—stupidly, she thought—and then placing it back in his own lap. He cocked his head at her, as if she were the riddle of the week.

She was about to let the man in on her little secret, about to explain everything before it went any further, when another man's reflection in the mirror stopped her short. How long had he been standing there in the shadows? Had he seen Hendrick's hand on her cheek? His intent gray eyes were narrowed seductively. Vaguely she became aware of Hendrick's voice beside her. "What?" she asked, surprised to find that she was suddenly breathless.

"I said, it's your turn," Hendrick repeated.

Jenny felt disoriented and dazed. She watched the reflection behind her as she tried to figure out what Hendrick expected of her. "My turn?" she asked, her eyes never leaving the mirror that reflected the gray ones now staring unabashedly at her full, slightly parted lips.

"I told you my name, so now you tell me yours," Hendrick explained reasonably.

"Yes, yes, of course," she replied, totally under the spell of the misty-cloud eyes behind her. "It's Claudia," she lied.

The mirrored gray eyes were on her torso now, taking

The Family Plan 3

in every smooth inch of it with their thorough, sensual search. Slowly the man advanced, bringing his gaze to the level of hers in the mirror. Jenny wrapped her feet around the cylinder of the barstool and hung on for sweet life. She turned her head toward the man now standing directly behind her and was immediately lost in the smoky depths of his incendiary eyes.

"Dance?" he asked her.

The only dancing she ever did was to the early morning radio as she cleaned her house. "I–I'm a bit rusty in the joints," she confessed.

"We'll work the kinks out together," he promised.

Jenny was sliding off the high stool, inordinately drawn to the man.

"Hey!" Hendrick called, grabbing Jenny's arm. "Is this guy bothering you, Claudia?"

"Claudia?" The gray-eyed man smiled as he repeated the name with which Jenny had recently christened herself. "Very pretty."

"No, no, he's not," she assured Hendrick. She slid her arm out of Hendrick's grasp and wrapped her hands around the other man's neck, reveling in the sexy feel of the sinews and muscles under his healthy skin.

He drew her close in a daringly intimate way. His fine, long-boned hands slid slowly down her spine until they came to rest on the high curve of her buttocks. With a deliberate and lascivious move, he fit her body against his so that she could feel his arousal. An involuntary moan rose from deep within her throat. "What's your name, Mister?" she asked him.

"Mister," he answered smoothly, looking at her with half-closed eyes.

"Mister?" she echoed. "Whoever dubbed you that must have a sense of humor."

"She does. She knows a lot about appropriate names." He splayed his fingers across her bottom and drew tiny circles over her hipbones with his thumbs.

"You're a good dancer," Jenny complimented, feeling

her soft body melting into the protective nooks of his elbows, his chest, the inviting space between the length of his legs.

"Claudia," he whispered into Jenny's ear, "let's get out of here."

"Just a little longer," she coaxed. "You feel so good."

He ran one hand up her spine and cradled her back. "So do you," he answered throatily, adjusting his body against hers.

Something about his dancing seemed too sure, too practiced. It nagged at Jenny until she had to ask, "Do a lot of dancing, Mister?"

"Some," he responded, seemingly lost in the sensation of having her so near.

Jenny tried to repress the emotion boiling up in her. She tried to calm her questioning mind. She did so want this evening to be perfect. "I don't," she retorted, biting her disobedient tongue only after the words had escaped.

Mister fit one warm, strong hand around the back of her neck and began massaging one of her tensing shoulders. "We'll have to do something about that, won't we?" he whispered.

Jenny couldn't help it. She didn't want to feel this resentment, this anger, but she did. As though some apprenticing devil had thrown cold water on her, she pulled away from Mister and gave him a tight smile. "I'm leaving now," she informed him.

"Then so am I," he responded, obviously confused.

Jenny crossed the dance floor to get her coat off the rack. She gave an angry tug and her woolen jacket fell into her hands.

"He *is* bothering you, isn't he," Hendrick stated, suddenly behind her. His moustache fairly quivered with rage.

"Forget it," she commanded, but this time her threat was unheeded.

"I saw the way he treated you on the dance floor."

Jenny winced as she guessed what this patient operator had been thinking as he'd watched her and Mister.

"You're a nice person," he defended, "and I don't like

the way he acted so... grabby."

"Hendrick, please, I can take care of this," Jenny reasoned. Too late she saw the gray-eyed man approaching. "Mister!" she warned.

Hendrick turned to her. "You don't even know his name?" he exclaimed, obviously incredulous.

"That *is* my name," Mister put in, reaching for Jenny's arm and tugging her toward himself.

Hendrick stepped between them. "Hey listen, mister," he began, his proud chin pointing toward the other man. "If she wants to go anywhere with you, she'll say so."

"I do! I do!" Jenny interjected, pushing past Hendrick's taut body and trying to usher Mister away.

Hendrick's hand slapped down onto Mister's arm, seemingly stopping time and motion as the three of them waited for the other leaden shoe to drop. At the same moment, the band stopped playing to take a break. Jenny's ears felt peculiarly numb. The din in the bar seemed distant and remote as the two men exchanged threatening glances.

She vainly tried to pry Hendrick's hand off the other man's arm. "Hendrick, please," she pleaded. "I'm going of my own free will."

"You heard her," Mister asserted. "Now let go of me before I pluck that mouse off your lip."

"Mister, stop it!" Jenny advised sternly as she tried to wedge her body between the two steaming hulks. "He'll hit you!"

"That's not a bad idea, Claudia," Hendrick muttered. And before she could stop the action of Hendrick's powerful arm, his balled fist connected with Mister's eye.

"That's for a man who pushes a woman around," Hendrick contended.

He yanked his own jacket off the rack and stormed out of the now-quiet and awed bar.

The next morning, in the renovated kitchen of her rambling old house, Jenny was contrite. She scrambled the dozen eggs in her large skillet. She put both toasters to work at once—the pop-up one and the toaster oven. She fed apples from the tree in the yard into her heavy-duty juicer, and she brewed a pot of herbal tea on her industrial stove. She bit her lip as she worked, worrying the tender flesh with her nervousness.

"Ma, should I wear my coat today?" her seven-year-old son, Matthew, asked.

Jenny heaved an impatient sigh. "Matthew..." she began in a tone that told him he should know better.

"Okay, okay, I know. 'Call the weather number,'" he mimicked.

Jenny turned to face him. In spite of herself, she smiled. The small gesture made her son hug her hips. "Sorry, Mommy," he whispered into the folds of her tufted teal-blue satin robe.

Jenny smoothed his blond hair. "You kids run up a phone bill that would make a drunken sailor sober. If you can dial a friend's house, you can take care of the weather report," she reminded him.

Just then Amy, Jenny's ten-year-old, sauntered into the kitchen. "Yeah, Matthew," she taunted her younger brother. "Mommy and Daddy want us to be independent." She eyed Matthew's face pressed into Jenny's robe. "Not clinging vines! You know the deal. Mommy makes breakfast and lunches if we take responsibility for getting dressed."

Jenny hid an amused smile behind a palm that feigned a mission of catching a cough. Amy had certainly taken care of outfitting herself. She was in pink three-quarter-length ballet pants, a floppy red sweater belted with a green vinyl dog's leash, and white satin ballet shoes decorated with her own cubist renditions.

Matthew sulkily left his mother's side. After he passed Amy, he stuck his tongue out at her. Too tired to face the fireworks a reprimand would cause, Jenny turned away from the scene and tittered quietly. If Amy had seen Matthew's gesture, there would have been an early-morning riot in the Heath household—and the last thing Jenny needed right now was a major incident among the ranks.

The Family Plan 7

"Amy," she tried nonchalantly, "your brother has just turned seven. That makes him more than three years your junior." She turned from the fragrant eggs in butter to see her daughter's face. "Be a little patient, will you, honey?"

Amy looked up from the textbook she was perusing. "When I was seven I had to do everything for myself," she complained.

Jenny smiled softly at her studious but competitive child. "You all did," she reminded her. "Just give him time to catch up. He'll be doing everything for himself soon, too." Amy was the child for whom Jenny had to have the most love, the most patience, the most understanding.

Todd, who at eighteen was Jenny's oldest child, came bouncing into the kitchen, his headphones at a volume that allowed even the disc jockey's off-color jokes to reach Jenny's ears. "'Morning, Mother," he said, kissing her cheek and then plopping onto the bench seat along the window. He beat out a tune on the table. "Can I have just toast this morning? I gotta weigh in for wrestling today."

"Have just eggs," Jenny suggested, tipping the fluffy mound onto a huge yellow platter that matched her bright and homey kitchen.

The two older girls came into the kitchen together. Lately they'd been inseparable. Joyce, the fifteen-year-old, approached Jenny and took the eggs from her. Karen, the thirteen-year-old and the quietest of the Heath children, began buttering the growing stack of whole wheat toast.

Todd jumped up to check the baby's bottle, which was dancing in the boiling water. "Should I let him stay in the crib?" he asked his mother.

"Bring him downstairs, please. I'll change him in a minute."

"Where'd Daddy get the black eye?" Joyce asked as she doled out portions of the eggs.

Jenny wiped her hands on an apron tied to the refrigerator. "Black eye?" she stalled, hoping to find a suitable answer in the alleyways of her thoughts. "Didn't he tell you himself?" she hedged. She and her husband usually worked out details like this before they were confronted by the children. But last night... well, that had been so absolutely different from anything they'd ever done!

"He told me to ask someone named Claudia," Joyce said, wrinkling her pretty nose. Joyce was the picture of her handsome father. "But I got the feeling he was stalling, just like you are."

Amy giggled. Matthew, who copied everything Amy did, giggled too.

"You don't even know why you're laughing," Amy accused.

Joyce fitted her lace-edged prairie skirt around her thighs and sat down. "Well, neither do you, hotshot," she told Amy. "So don't act so big!"

"He had a little accident," Jenny began, turning away to get the baby's diaper and lotion from the cabinet above the sink.

"Why'd you two go out so late?" Joyce persisted.

Jenny put a hand to her forehead, remembering the topsy-turvy scene at the bar in Adler. Adler was a town known for its gin mills, unlike the refined village of Piper where the Heaths' lived. She leaned back against the counter. When Todd rejoined the group with the crying baby, she had all six children assembled, eagerly awaiting her explanation. She chuckled and then said sternly, "It's none of your business—any of you."

When Jenny's husband walked in, the entire family was silent in a showdown of stares and counter-stares.

"Just coffee for me, dear," he said as he took his place at the head of the table. He smiled at his children, who simply regarded him with curious stillness. "What's the matter?" he asked. "Haven't you ever seen a black eye before? You watch enough television to acclimate yourselves to violence."

There was silence.

"What does acclimate mean?" Matthew finally asked.

"Get used to," Amy answered.

"Wow!" Joyce exclaimed. "*I* didn't even know that."

The Family Plan   9

"Eat your breakfast," Jenny ordered. Automatically her children began forking their food.

Todd was still staring. His father put his coffee cup down and stared right back. "I asked you if you'd ever seen a black eye," he reminded his son.

Todd took off his earphones, which had been blessedly silent since he'd gone to get the baby. "Not on an art dealer in a business suit," he countered.

Suddenly, his father's fist hit the table. "Jenny! Do you ever get the feeling that we're tyrannized by our own children?"

Jenny slinked into a chair and looked into her beloved husband's gray eyes. "All the time," she responded, hoping he'd understand something of what she'd been complaining about lately—her sense of being trapped while he was free.

"Tyrannized!" Amy exploded. "You two get to do anything you want. *We're* the oppressed ones around here!"

Matthew was clearly about to side with his adored sister, but he stopped his retort in mid-breath, evidently realizing that he didn't understand the conversation.

"Adults!" Joyce exclaimed. "I can't wait to be one. I'll show you how you've been wasting your freedom!"

Todd nodded in agreement. "I think you two have this out of perspective," he began. "Now, if you saw things—"

"Who taught these kids to be so articulate?" Jenny's husband demanded.

"You did. You always insisted upon it, Mister," she retorted, feeling slightly mischievous as she used her secret and loving term for him.

"Watch out!" Todd said. "When she starts calling him that, the kissing starts." He grabbed his books and wagged a teasing finger at them before he handed the baby over to Jenny. "Careful, Mother, or you'll never get out of diapers!" He winked and ran out of the house before Jenny could catch her breath to reprimand him. Being a senior in high school had certainly made him bolder and more worldly.

"What'd he mean?" Amy asked, bewildered.

"Even *I* know that," Matthew boasted. He whispered to

his sister, "Kissing gives you babies." Then, obviously pleased with his announcement, he added, "Stupid!"

"It does not!" Amy insisted, horrified.

"Yes it does!" Matthew insisted.

The bus was outside, beeping its squeaky horn.

"Does not!" Amy insisted, looking more and more concerned as she gathered up her books.

Joyce and Karen, who were snickering, were already at the door. "'Bye, Mommy! Bye, Daddy!'" they called.

Jenny jumped up, baby in arms, to comfort Amy. Matthew was trying to kiss the baby good-bye, tugging on his little feet until Jenny had to stoop. "Don't worry, Amy," she told her daughter, "kissing doesn't give you babies."

At Amy's extraordinary sigh of relief, Jenny queried nervously, "Why? Have you been kissing anyone?"

Amy waved her mother's voice down. "'Bye! The bus'll leave without me," she said, rushing out the door that led directly to the driveway.

"You're only ten years old!" Jenny called frantically after her. "For heaven's sake, act like a kid!"

She fit the baby over her hip and stood staring after her children. Absently she asked Mister, "Do you think I should have a talk with her?"

"Amy? I wouldn't worry about her. She's a very intelligent girl."

"It's the studious ones you have to watch out for," Jenny reminded her husband. Then, as the bus pulled away from the yellowing fall lawn, she said, "Do you think she'll take after your sister Miriam? I mean, being intelligent hasn't done *her* any good. She has two master's degrees, one doctorate, and just as many children. And she's never been married!"

"Jenny," Mister said as he stretched up to his full formidable height. "They're all gone. We can start the kissing now." He wrapped her securely in his arms.

"What? And make more babies?"

As his soft, heated lips fell onto his wife's, he murmured, "Someone ought to have a talk with *you*. Preferably Amy.

The Family Plan 11

She knows kissing doesn't give you babies."

Jenny felt the powerful encouragement of Mister's tender lips. She fell under their spell the way she always did, sinking deeper and deeper into the enchantment with each excruciatingly soft touch of his moist, full mouth on hers.

Mister's familiar lips opened hers to admit his gentle tongue. Like a flower giving nectar to a bee, Jenny spread the petals of her body and drew him closer. A seething fire sparked and crackled in her soul at her husband's sexy probings.

The baby started to cry as Jenny's hold on him became tighter. Catapulted back into the world of reality, Jenny shook free of her husband's embrace and hurried the baby into the bathroom, where there was a large dressing table that had been built for the Heaths when they'd first bought the house more than ten years ago.

She began to wash and dress him, working furiously until Mister appeared at the door.

"What's wrong?" he asked. "Rushing for a train or something?"

Jenny slowed her hands and shook her head no.

"I was just trying to pick up where we left off last night," Mister murmured.

Jenny sighed as she reached for a presoaked cloth with which to clean her youngest child. "Mister," she began, "last night didn't go as well as you might think." She looked up in time to see Mister's one fully opened eye blink at her in amazement.

"Who's got the shiner to prove it, *Claudia?*" he demanded.

Jenny returned her attention to snapping the clean romper onto the baby. She smiled at his cooings and wrinkled her nose at him, shaking her blond curls to tumble within his reach. Delighted shrieks came out of his puckered little mouth.

"What I mean is, it started again—while we were dancing," she confessed, "that ugly feeling that you have a life so completely—" She yelped as the baby yanked on her hair. Mister gently extricated the tendrils and took the baby from his wife.

When he said nothing, she continued, "Well, for instance, you *dance*. How many men do you dance with?"

Mister did a double take. "I never dance with men," he protested.

"Then you see my point. You dance with a lot of women," she said as they returned to the kitchen.

"I do," Mister admitted as he held out a piece of dry toast for the baby to nibble.

"Watch that he doesn't choke on it," Jenny muttered before continuing. "It makes me feel insecure, Mister," she asserted. "You're always traveling around without me— Spain, Italy, England. And next month, China. My word! I can't even use my wok without burning the ginger, and my husband's going to China."

Mister reached for her, but his palms were full of mushy toast bits. As a compromise, he stroked her cheek with the back of his hand. "Do we have to go through this again?" he asked, clearly begging to change the subject.

"Yes, we do," Jenny said, half of her feeling like the Grinch who stole Christmas and the other half feeling justified. "When will you get it through your logical, well-adjusted mind that you've married a volatile, fiery woman? When will you acknowledge that I have real fears? Reasonable or un-, they're real."

"Sh, darling. I'm sorry you feel this way. I truly am. But what am I to do? Set fire to the house and ship the children to reform school?"

She could tell he was losing patience with her. "Lloyd," she said, calling him by the name she usually used only in the company of others. "Take last night."

Mister groaned and put a cupped, crumb-covered palm to his eye. "All your fault!" he teased.

"All I wanted was a taste of the intrigue you have almost every day of your life," Jenny defended. "It was good old American imagination that dreamed up that fictitious date. Imagine it—it could have been very exciting!" She tried in vain to hide her sense of delight from her husband.

"Wretch!" he joked. "You enjoyed that bruiser's attentions."

Jenny was laughing. "No," she managed. "I really and truly didn't. In fact, I tried to discourage him."

"With his calloused hand on your cheek?" Mister teased.

Now a new feeling was playing in the fields of Jenny's heart. "Mister?" she probed. "Were you jealous? C'mon, admit it. You wanted to deck Hendrick, didn't you?"

Mister shrugged and wiped the baby's mouth. He patted him on his diapered bottom and set him to crawl on the shiny yellow-tiled floor. "I trust you," he said simply.

"You see?" Jenny took the opportunity to point out. "You never have to worry about me. I'm a homebody, a salesman's lady-of-the-house, a dyed-in-the-poodle-wool mother and wife. But you! Why, just look at you, Mister. As I was reprimanding that poor man last night, I get a glimpse of your wonderful face in the mirror and I turn to...to..." She stared at her husband's hands. "Wet toast!" she finished. Then she slapped her own forehead. "See? Even my metaphors are domestic! Even as a strange man was playing up to me in a bar, I behaved like somebody's wife—or mother," she added vehemently.

Mister was at the sink, washing his well-formed, strong hands. "Darling, just because your experiment failed..."

"Oh, Mister, I did so want it to work. I wanted to meet you in a back-alley bar and have us get into a secret seduction. I wanted us to ache for each other the way we did before the six precious, precocious children, the two tempermental, if expensive, cars, and this huge, impossible-to-keep-clean house, and...oh, Mister, don't you see that every time I think I'm going to be free I get pregnant instead?"

Mister was suddenly on his knees beside her. His eyes narrowed sexily, his clean-shaven face and rich fragrance flooding her senses. She wanted to reach out and wrap her arms around him. "Some deep psychological sabotage?" he whispered mischievously.

Jenny stared at him intently. "Get off your knees; you're ruining the crease in your pants," she muttered. Then she added, "Is it?"

"What? Do you sabotage yourself?" Mister asked, brushing crumbs from his sports jacket in a way that infuriated Jenny. He always brushed himself off before he went out to greet the world. Any moment now and he'd be through the door, leaving her to cope with all the problems and details of running a household.

"No," she chided good-naturedly, "I was wondering if *you've* been the *saboteur*." At Mister's shocked expression she asked, "Why do we have children spaced just far enough apart to always keep me in talcum powder? And why won't you let me come to China with you next month?" She held up a very shiny copper frying pan and, using it as a mirror, adjusted her hair. "Am I so atrocious? Do I have a deficient vocabulary? Goo-goo, ga-ga?" she asked. Mister was laughing at her antics. "Is there a poster in the post office claiming I'm a flasher?" Jenny finished.

Mister scooped her off her feet and sat her on the counter top of her cheery kitchen. His lips fell on hers with a sweetness that communicated his deep affection. "You're perfect," he whispered into her open mouth. "Even Hendrick recognized that."

Jenny pushed Mister so hard that he bumped against the cooking island in the center of the room. "Answer me!" she demanded, at wit's end. She hopped off the counter.

"Jenny," Mister said in a soft and reasonable voice, "you're involved in every aspect of my life. You *are* my life. You're the reason I do any of my work. Which, I have to add, is not as glamorous as you insist upon believing. You're the reason I dance with other women—very rich ones, who have an appreciation for art—"

"Stop!" she said. "You're making my husband sound like the gigolo he'd better not ever become—for me *or* my children."

"Darling," Mister said, gathering her into his arms and burrowing his face into her neck. "I have an unconventional job, that's all. I don't sell to the man in the street; I depend upon private presentations in people's homes or in museums or institutions looking to invest in art. And the hours—why, they're perfect for a family man. I'm right here in town more than I'm away, and—look at this—it's almost nine and I still haven't left the house."

She knew that he was right, that he did run a very demanding and offbeat business, that some of his work took place out of town—in big cities all over the States and in big cities everywhere else in the world. When he worked in his gallery in Piper, the nature of what he did gave him the freedom to attend to his family. But when he went away, he was away, and they had only their daily phone chats.

"I know, I know," Jenny affirmed. "I don't want to complain. I have no right to complain. But, Mister,"—she leaned her head against his chest—"I miss it. I want to be out there, too. I want to be with you, or," she hastily corrected herself, "at least feel that I have an existence other than the one inside this house."

Mister raised his eyebrows helplessly. "Care to switch places? You go make the living and I'll take care of our children?"

Jenny knew that it would probably take years before she could earn enough to support a family of eight. She bit into Mister's jacket in frustration. "I have a better idea. Let's tie them on silk leashes and leave them each a bowl of water," she said, laughing at the ludicrous image her suggestion conjured up. "Then we'll run off together!"

Mister whacked her on the bottom. Her robe flew open as she reached to defend her vulnerable posterior. "You're wicked," Mister whispered as his lips bit passionately into her throat. "And someday I'm going to make that little barroom fantasy of yours come true. You'll be an unattached, desirable woman in a bar, and I'll come along to seduce you to the dance floor." He gave a small laugh. "Didn't take much cajoling last night," he mused aloud. "Then I'll talk you into spending the night with me in a hotel."

Jenny reached down to pick up the baby, who was trying to climb up her long, flyaway robe. "The kind with mirrors on the ceiling?" she asked, encouraging Mister in this reverie.

He nodded and nuzzled the baby, who gave a crackly little laugh. Then he playfully bit Jenny's nose and the baby's. He pulled them to himself and gave them a fetching smile. When he pulled away, he brushed his sports jacket off.

"Will you please stop doing that?" Jenny demanded. "I'm always afraid you'll be walking out the door any second."

"I will be," he assured her, giving her one of his distracted parting pecks.

She stamped her foot, scaring the poor baby, who looked up in astonishment. As she comforted him, she heard the door close.

Within moments Mister was tapping at the window. Jenny straddled the bench near the table and opened the window high, shielding the baby in a fold of her robe.

"Doesn't the housekeeper come today?" Mister asked her.

"She'll be here any minute."

"Good. Meet me in town for lunch."

Jenny looked at the baby. "What about baby Lloyd?" she asked. "You know he's too young for a sitter. I'm still nursing twice a day until I get him weaned."

Mister winked and shrugged. "Does he like bean sprouts?"

"Oh. We're going to the health bar?"

"Where else would my wife allow me to eat?"

"Well, it's just that when a woman gets invited out to lunch, she wants to taste something other than what she can cook herself."

"Does he eat Mexican food?" Mister asked, winking at the baby.

Jenny shook her head no but agreed to the rendezvous. "I'll meet you at the Mexican restaurant at noon." She pretended to whisper in order to keep the baby from understanding. "I'll feed him at home first."

"You're a smart mother," Mister complimented.

"It's hereditary. I get it from Amy."

Mister laughed at the joke and tweaked the baby's nose. "Don't be late!" he called as he approached the silver sports car.

"I always am!" Jenny retorted. "No housekeeper alone can absolve the sins of a family of eight in only one day a week."

"Give her another day, too," Mister returned as his car's smooth engine purred to life.

"No use trying that now," Jenny answered. "Not as long as I'm still at home with the baby." She muttered the next words. "May as well keep myself busy."

"What?" Mister called, sticking his head out the car window.

"Have a better day, Mister!" Jenny said, laughing at her ease with Todd's latest expression.

Mister threw her a kiss and backed out of the driveway into the proverbial stream of life.

2

JENNY WAS RUNNING LATE, as usual. She scooped up the clean laundry and ran through the house, depositing it in her children's bedrooms for them to put away themselves. She ended in the master bedroom, where Bea Kirke, the housekeeper, was changing the sheets on the king-size bed.

"That's okay, Jenny," the kindly woman said. "You run along and meet Mister Lloyd. I'll finish up here."

"No, you'll never get done by four if someone doesn't pick up the loose ends. Details! Details!" Jenny ranted as she threw clean towels into the master bath and switched on the shower. She then ran to leave sheets in Todd's room.

When Jenny came back into her bedroom, Bea was standing with her hands on her hips. "At least leave baby Lloyd for me to watch. He won't be any trouble."

Jenny loved her housekeeper. A big, strong woman who had a very bad family life, Beatrice Kirke was one of the most sincere and helpful human beings Jenny had ever known. Since the Heaths had moved to Piper, when Amy was born, the housekeeper had been there, like a warm and comforting grandmother.

"No, Bea," Jenny said, yanking on a stray lock of blond hair that fell over her eyes. "You have enough to worry about without having a potential time bomb go off under your coccyx."

Bea gave one of her endearing chuckles. "He's a good boy," she defended.

"Until he wakes up and finds his mother gone," Jenny reminded her, thinking about two times she'd gone into town to do errands and left baby Lloyd with Bea.

"He was only a baby then," the housekeeper protested, rumpling the sheets into a manageable ball.

"That was only last month," Jenny said sardonically before heading into the bathroom.

Once she was in the shower, Jenny had the chance to be disconnected from her worries. The hot, soothing torrents running down her fit body made her feel deliciously languorous. She scrubbed her peachy skin until a warm glow heated her some more, and then she lavished her long, curly hair with a fragrant, expensive shampoo. She took her time about letting the stream of hot water rinse the suds away, allowing her heavy, wet hair to trail down her back.

After drying off, she dressed casually, choosing gray pants and a long tunic that covered her hips. Ever since Matthew's birth, Jenny's body had changed. Where she used to complain about boyish hips, she now had curves that were too full and rounded for her taste. Oh, Mister liked them well enough. He thought his wife had the sexiest body in the world.

Smiling, Jenny recalled the revealing outfit she'd worn last night. Last night had been one big, glorious fantasy come true. Well, almost. She had been determined to leave her domesticity and motherliness at home, planning to encounter the man she loved on new turf. She had wanted to let him see her in another light—as a woman, pure and simple—not his wife or his mate or the mother of his children.

She let the blow dryer fluff up her hair, leaning so far forward that her forehead almost touched her knees. Proud of the progress her body had been making since she'd joined yoga classes two years ago, she wrapped one slender arm around the back of her calves and pulled her head closer. For the first time, she actually touched her hairline to her unbent knee.

Elated, she added the small accomplishment to her list of things to tell Mister. She quickly readied the baby, who was being blessedly cooperative, gave Bea instructions to take a break and have some lunch, and flew out to her station wagon.

It was a wonderfully clear day, one of those days that seemed like a stage designer's fabrication. The sky was so blue it looked painted. The foliage was at the peak of fall coloring, with some trees mimicking the brilliance of flames. The roads were dark black, and the yellow birch leaves fell like fairy snow from the woods along the drive into town.

Jenny caught the mood of the day; she felt revitalized and fresh. An inordinately gay sensation built up in her as she looked forward to seeing Mister and having a private little lunch with him. Just the two of them alone at last. She looked over to baby Lloyd's car seat. "Sorry, kid. Forgot about you," she teased the sleepy child. His head bobbed once, and his little hands and feet thrashed in an unnecessary effort to right himself. Soon the motion of the car rocked him to sleep.

Once they reached the restaurant, Jenny checked her tweed shawl at the coat room and proceeded to scan the faces of the diners. She didn't know why she should get so excited about simply seeing the back of Mister's head after all these years, but the fact was that she did.

A geyser of love sprang up from the well deep within her. She couldn't wipe the ridiculous grin off her face as she made her way through the crowd. But just as she cleared an old brick piling that decorated the rustic restaurant, she caught sight of a woman's head leaning toward Mister's.

She stopped walking and adjusted the baby in the car caddy she carried. For a split second she experienced a horrible pang of jealousy as she took in the woman's sleek black hair that flowed down behind the chair back, probably reaching to her waist or beyond.

It didn't take long for Jenny to muster up her acute sense of rationality. She took a deep breath, reprimanding herself for the foolish emotion the woman's presence elicited from her. "Come off it, Guinevere," she muttered to herself. Her what-to-name-baby memory instantly supplied the translation of her name: fair lady. If the fair lady in question came apart over a clump of black hair, how would she behave when the owner of the hair got a face?

The face attached to the hair was, Jenny hated to admit, one of the most exotic and beautiful she'd ever seen—a perfect blend of Eastern and Western features. Of course, Jenny reasoned, the dramatic use of black to outline the hazel eyes contributed to the smoky effect. Still, this woman would probably look good in the sweaty sauna of Todd's high school gym.

"Darling," Mister said as he rose to greet Jenny and take the baby from her.

Jenny began to settle herself in a seat across from the other woman and Mister.

"No, no, no, sit here," Mister instructed, relinquishing the chair he'd been in. He winked at his wife. "I want the pleasure of gazing at two beauties during lunch."

Cute, Mister, Jenny thought. Want a twin brother for your bruised eye?

He placed the baby's stiff seat across two chairs as he introduced the women. "Heddy Lock, this is my wife, Guinevere Heath. But you can call her Jenny like the rest of us do."

Jenny extended a hand as she surveyed the other woman. At close range, Jenny decided Heddy's looks would survive even a mud-wrestling match. "How do you do?" Jenny murmured politely.

The other woman was smiling so broadly that her lustrous teeth picked up the dim light from the candle in the centerpiece. "Oh, I'm so happy to meet you! Lloyd's been raving about his lovely wife for years." She immediately turned to run a hand across the sleeping baby's brow. "And the children," she added.

Was the woman stupid? Jenny wondered. Didn't she know enough to let sleeping babies lie? If baby Lloyd woke up, Jenny would let him sit on Heddy's lap through lunch!

"Thank you," Jenny replied, a bit too stiffly. "I wish I could say the same." The last bit came out before she could censor it. Such impulsiveness was the product of underexposure to the civilized world, she rationalized.

Mister shot her an annoyed glance. "You remember my telling you about Heddy, Jenny. She's the expert on Chinese Imperial art. I've gone to all her seminars, and we worked together on the acquisition for the museum in Texas."

Jenny did remember, but she had never connected a face to her husband's remarks on the other woman's scholarly achievements. "Vaguely," she muttered as she took a menu from the waitress, who asked if Jenny wanted a cocktail. Both Mister and Heddy were drinking. "Yes," she answered. "I'll have what they're drinking."

"But—" Mister began to protest. A quick sharp glance from him told Jenny that he knew what she was about. He gave a tiny laugh and shook his head. She never drank, but today she'd try to match moves with Heddy.

It was a silly impulse, even a degrading one, but Jenny simply couldn't control it. An unreasonable jealousy seethed deep within her. "Are you in Piper often, Miss Lock?" Jenny asked. Her first mistake. Call her Heddy.

"Call me Heddy," she answered. "No, I've come to make the arrangements for Lloyd's trip."

Mister unfolded his menu and looked over it to his wife's eyes. "I tried to call you about an hour ago to warn you it would be a business lunch, but no one answered," he said, clearly hinting for her to keep her head and be mindful of his professional relationship with Heddy.

"I was hiding in the shower," Jenny explained, "and Bea's head was probably stuffed in the laundry."

Heddy began to laugh at the way Jenny phrased herself. Jenny suddenly remembered that many people used to think her very entertaining. People outside her family. People to whom she was still a mystery. "Oh, that sounds like such luxury," Heddy remarked, still laughing.

"What? Dirty laundry?" Jenny asked, knowing full well what the other woman meant.

Heddy reached across the table to touch Mister's sleeve. "Lloyd, she's so funny!"

Have I left the room? Jenny thought. How could Heddy take such a liberty with Jenny's husband and then talk about *her* in the third person?

"I meant the late-morning shower," Heddy said. "I'm up, showered, and out of the house by eight."

"Well, I'm up, unshowered, and never out of the house by six," Jenny retorted. "Except to lug out garbage pails." Heddy was almost doubled over in laughter.

Jenny caught Mister's reprimanding eye and wished she could stop her fool tongue from wagging like a daffy dog's tail. But all the caged feelings she'd been experiencing were suddenly and inexorably surfacing. She tried a civil approach. "Where are you staying?" she managed.

"At the Lady K," Heddy replied. "It's a dream."

Jenny nodded. She was doing fine. "Yes, Lloyd and I sometimes dine there." Had she said *dine?* Whatever happened to good old-fashioned *eating?*

"I hope you'll come join me one evening," Heddy invited. "We'll sit on the park side. I always do for dinner. You can watch such glorious sunsets. I usually have breakfast on the golf course side, because the sunshine is so pleasant in the morning."

Jenny smiled. How bad could a woman who worshipped the sun be? And her taste wasn't bad. After all, she did find Jenny amusing. Jenny chided herself for having had such ignoble impulses about Heddy. It seemed she was getting rusty at handling adults, and the knowledge further frustrated her. Well, she'd try, for the remainder of lunch at least, to open her mouth without stuffing her shoe leather into it.

Heddy turned her hazel eyes to Jenny and tilted her

delicate face, sending a mass of hair cascading over one shoulder.

What was in those gorgeous orbs? Could it be a genuine sincerity? Real niceness?

"How many children do you have? I don't mean to sound clichéd, but you look so young." She pointed a long, delicate finger at Mister. "Lloyd, aren't you worried with such a young wife?" she teased familiarly.

Of course she was on friendly terms with Mister; they'd been colleagues long enough.

Jenny and Mister were practically the same age. She was thirty-eight and he was thirty-nine. But it was true that Mister had graying temples, while Jenny's hair was still a lustrous, natural blond streaked with amber. The hard work and extreme financial pressures during their first eight years of marriage had taken their toll on Mister. But to Jenny, her husband was still the most exciting and handsome man in the world. Surely other women noticed his deeply sensual eyes, his expressive, full lips, his extraordinarily generous personality.

Lloyd momentarily feigned injury at Heddy's unwitting insult, then he immediately laughed and began singing his wife's praises. He was about to give Heddy the number of children he and Jenny had been surviving when he stopped in mid-sentence.

Jenny followed his gaze to the men's room door. Todd was jamming a comb into his back pocket and making his way toward a table in the corner. Jenny let out an audible gasp.

"What's wrong?" Heddy asked, turning to follow their surprised gazes. "Do you know that young man?"

Todd looked up just in time to see the three adults gaping at him. The woman he was about to join noticed them, too.

Jenny turned away so that they wouldn't see her release a laugh. That Todd! Wrestling weigh-in, indeed. She'd instinctively named him correctly when she'd been looking through the name books before his birth. Todd. Latin origin. Meaning: the fox.

"Isn't he supposed to be in school?" Mister snapped, throwing his napkin onto the table and beginning to get up. Todd evidently knew better than to have his father approach him; he coaxed his girlfriend up and began what to him must have seemed like his last mile.

"School?" Heddy asked.

Jenny couldn't resist. "My husband's a truant officer when he's not busy being a cultured member of the intelligentsia," she explained, smirking at the couple who were now beside the table.

"Um," Todd began. "Peggy," he tried. "This is, um..." As though he'd forgotten something, Todd bent his handsome, if red, face to Jenny and kissed her solemnly, his eyes pleading with her to get him out of this embarrassing mess. "Hi, *Jenny,*" Todd said, clearly hoping she'd pick up his lead and not expose him to this woman who, though young, was obviously at least a few years older than he.

Jenny stalled. "Peggy," she mused aloud. "Greek in origin. A diminutive of Margaret, meaning the pearl. Very fitting, don't you think, Lloyd?"

Mister glanced from his wife to his son to the pert and pretty young Peggy. Jenny could see him struggling with the impulse to get up and take his son by the ear. In the commotion of first-name introductions, she managed to whisper, "Don't, Mister. Please." He first did a double take as though she were mad, but then his stern eyes softened with calm amusement. There'd be time at dinner tonight to carve the turkey.

Mister put his hand out. "Good to see you again, Todd," he said. He then graciously shook Peggy's hand. "Peggy." He nodded. The young woman circled the table to the baby, who had finally awakened. He had that dopey, sleepy look that Jenny so loved—like a nutty professor who never came out of the clouds. His feathery hair was crushed and messy from having been in the bunting hood. "Oh!" Peggy exclaimed, with that how-I-envy-mothers look in her eye. "Is he yours, Jenny?"

Jenny nodded proudly and looked from Mister to Todd.

The Family Plan 27

"Your first?" Peggy asked.

Todd's smile fell with such speed Jenny thought she heard it clatter on the table. She threw a nonchalant hand into the air. "Well..." she began.

"No," Mister finished. "Not exactly." He cast a comical but stern look at his eighteen-year-old son. "It's been so long, Todd," Mister said. "How old are you now? I mean..." He shrugged, his unbearably handsome face pretending innocence.

Jenny pressed one high heel into the toe of Mister's shoe. He shook it free.

"I'm twenty-one," Todd responded. "Sir," he added hastily.

"Twenty-one, eh?" Mister repeated, using his suave, professional manners. "Seems like only this morning you were eighteen. Doesn't time fly, Jenny?"

"I never even notice time," Jenny murmured. "What with taking care of my five children."

"Five?" both Peggy and Heddy echoed in astonishment.

"Would have been six, but we lost one to old age."

Evidently neither of the women thought it polite to ask the nature of Jenny and Lloyd's tragedy.

"Well, um," Todd was saying, "the waiter has brought our food, so, um, we, um, let's go, Peggy, okay?"

"Don't eat too much!" Jenny warned. "Wrestling!"

With quick and awkward good-byes, the young couple took their leave.

"Handsome young man," Heddy Lock remarked.

"Looks like his father did at that age," Jenny said.

"Are you related to him or something?" Heddy inquired. "He resembles you a bit, Lloyd."

"He ought to. He's my son."

"Oh." Heddy was clearly at a loss. Gingerly she added, "From a former marriage?"

For some reason Heddy's innocent remark had Jenny laughing with mirth. "No, he's mine, too," she said.

Heddy looked into Jenny's eyes to be sure she wasn't kidding. "You two lost no time!" she exclaimed.

"We were married when I turned twenty. That's too young, don't you think?" Jenny asked as she took her drink from the cocktail waitress, who asked if they were ready to see their regular waiter.

"No thank you," Mister told her. "I have a feeling we'll all be here a long time."

"Not too long, I hope," Jenny said. "At the rate our son is aging, he'll need dentures and a cane by dessert!"

"He's only eighteen," Mister explained to Heddy, who seemed intrigued by the turn of events.

"But you look so young!" Heddy told Jenny.

"How young?" she challenged playfully.

Heddy laughed. "Well, actually you do look thirty-five or somewhere around there, and that would figure well with Todd's age, but somehow you're a very young thirty-five or -seven or whatever you are." She directed her hazel eyes at Jenny. "You know what I mean. The thirties are the years when a woman can look ageless or... washed-up."

"A man, too!" Mister put in, obviously referring to Heddy's earlier comment about his age.

Heddy looked at Mister, seeming to ponder the remark. "You certainly don't look washed-up, but you are a more definitive late thirties or early forties."

"Thirty-nine," he clarified.

"And you?" Jenny felt comfortable enough to ask as she perused the menu replete with tiny drawings of Mexican cities. "You're also an ageless thirty-something."

"Thirty-three."

"Have you any children?"

"No. I've been married twice, but I've been too involved in my career to think of them. They seem such a burden—"

Just as Heddy's eyes widened in apparent embarrassment over having said such a thing to a mother of six children, baby Lloyd began crying.

"Here, give him to me," Jenny directed Mister, surrendering to the irony.

"I—I'm sorry," Heddy began.

"Don't be," Jenny assured her. "There are days when I wonder if—" She stopped talking as she stared blankly across the room to where Todd and his lady friend sat engaged in a serious conversation. Something about their demeanors seemed so intimate, and for a moment she sensed she was losing her son. Then she focused on her husband's face. He seemed to be waiting for her to finish her sentence, but she restrained herself from voicing her recent feelings of disenchantment over being solely a wife and mother.

"I've been such a klutz, I'm afraid," Heddy was saying. "I'm usually not this insensitive, believe me." Her hand was on Jenny's arm near where baby Lloyd's head lay.

"You're not insensitive at all, Heddy," Jenny told her. "In fact, in a strange way I feel we were destined to meet."

"How's that?" Mister asked, reaching over to wriggle the baby's stockinged toe.

"I've been feeling so isolated." She looked up at Heddy, who had, since the incident with Todd, become just another woman and not a terrible threat. "And you seem so accomplished, which I'd like to be."

Heddy looked pensive for a moment. When she spoke, it was carefully, as she wanted both to be specific and to avoid being a "klutz." "Every time I've thought of having children and having a conventional marriage, that very same sensation wells up in me. I feel I'd be so isolated. But then—it's strange—there are also times when I think I've convinced myself of that precisely because I have, so far, made the decision *not* to have them." She watched as baby Lloyd sucked on the breadstick in his mother's hand. "Isn't that odd? I'd never put it in those terms before."

Mister heaved a sigh that had both women looking at him. He winked at them and shook his head. "When are you women going to realize that everything in life is a trade-off, a compromise?" He looked at Jenny with a certain softness and compassion. "Would you have life any other way?"

"You can bet your golf clubs and tennis shoes I would!"

The simple remark made the three of them laugh.

"Listen," Mister said, "we're all at that terrible age when we start questioning what we've done so far with our lives. It's scary to be Jenny, who feels that so much of her fate and life is sealed, and it's scary to be Heddy, who feels that her chances for having children are diminishing with every year, and it's scary to be me, who is so hungry that if we don't order soon, I'm going to show my violent side and topple this table!"

"Is that how you got that black eye? From being hungry?" Heddy asked.

"No," Jenny put in. *"I* was the hungry one then."

"Okay," Heddy conceded, showing her dainty palms. "Family joke, obviously."

They ordered a hearty lunch and enjoyed a good conversation throughout it. The talk turned to business, and even though Jenny did not take an active part in her husband's art world, she understood enough about it to recognize important names, dates, and artists.

"I want to get my hands on some vases from the Ming dynasty," Mister told Heddy.

"Don't worry," she assured him. "I have a connection in a most unlikely village in the mountains. He once told me that he could get me at least two of them if I had the right buyer. He speaks only Chinese."

"Listen," Jenny said, "translated into English, 'right buyer' means 'lots of won ton dough.' And I thought I couldn't speak Chinese!" she winked at Mister as he laughingly shook his head at her. "Hey, neither can you," she reminded him, wondering how he'd make such an important deal without an interpreter.

"That's where I come in," Heddy informed her.

"You're going, too?" Jenny asked. She wasn't so much jealous as she was surprised. At this point she was feeling a warm trust for the other woman.

"She's invaluable for this trip. I thought I mentioned it to you."

Jenny yanked her finger out of the baby's mouth as his hard gums came down on it. "You probably did—as I was

The Family Plan 31

knee deep in a bathroom flood or something."

"I'm very excited," Heddy said. "It's been almost a year."

"You were there last year?"

"She's the one who sent me those Buddhist prayer flags and *mani* stones from occupied Tibet," Mister explained.

Jenny grimaced as she thought about how much she'd love to go traveling to exotic ports around the world. There was always something that kept her tied to her family and house. "Don't say any more," she warned Heddy. "I have a very jealous nature."

"Of Lloyd?" Heddy laughed as if she thought Jenny had suggested the most ridiculous thing in the world. "He's a kitten—a real family man, a genuine article loyalist!" Heddy asserted.

"Hey, don't make me sound so bland!" Mister protested.

"Oh, Mister," Jenny said, "you couldn't be bland if I soaked you in milk for three days." Then she caught herself. "You see? *All* my metaphors are domestic! I mean, I managed to get an education after Mister got his, so I'm not exactly an ingenue, but my experience is—well, there's no other way to put it—as exciting as a dirty mop."

Jenny enjoyed the laughter she was eliciting from her husband and his business associate. She was eager to please them, to feel a part of what they felt. She had confidence in herself, it was true, but she felt she lacked a certain mystery—the kind of mystery that lurked behind Heddy's smoky eyes or Hendrick's sexy moustache. Heddy and Hendrick. Not only did she know little about the kind of people they were, she also knew little about their names. One of the kids must have ripped the *H* pages out of her baby books!

"Actually, I wasn't trying to say I was jealous of Mister," Jenny told Heddy. "Although I have to admit that when I saw him sitting with a beautiful black-haired woman, my blood boiled. But you're right—I should trust him by now. He's such a devoted man." She looked at her husband, who gave her one of his cut-the-story-short smirks, and then said, "What really bothers me is that other people are always having all the fun."

Just then the waiter brought a red phone to the table. "Mrs. Heath? A Mrs. Kirke on the line."

Startled, Jenny took the receiver. "Bea?"

"I'm sorry to be bothering you when you and Mister Lloyd are finally alone..."

Jenny smiled wryly, fluttering her lashes at Heddy.

"...but the school called here to tell you that Amy fell and needs some stitches in her lip."

"How, Bea? When?" Jenny asked, ready to stand up and run.

"Just this minute. The nurse has ice on it—"

"Okay. Okay. I'll see you later. Thanks."

She picked up the baby, explained the situation, and flew out of the restaurant with Mister on her heels. "No, no, it's all right. Go back inside. It's just some stitches. We've had broken bones and broken hearts; this is nothing. Go back. Tell Heddy to come for dinner some night."

When she finally got home at three forty-five, Jenny was exhausted. The baby had cried through the entire wait in the emergency room, Amy had been afraid because it had been her first visit to the hospital since her birth, and the doctor who'd treated her had hardly spoken enough English to allow Amy to understand the simple things he'd required of her.

"My Amy," Jenny soothed as she helped her daughter get out of her blood-stained clothes. "My sweet, lovable Amy." The child simply lay her listless head on her mother's shoulder as Jenny unclasped the green leash from around her waist and got her ready for a nap. She'd named this one right, too. Amy: lovable.

By the time Amy was in bed, Jenny was too worn out to fight the baby's crying, so she went against her resolve to nurse him only twice a day and sneaked into the den to nurse. The softness and warmth of something he missed during this weaning period immediately calmed him, and Jenny felt a pang of doubt over ending his nursing so soon. All she'd have to do would be to suckle him more often

The Family Plan

and she'd have all the milk he required. Why be in such a rush to deny her child something he so desperately wanted? Sometimes she felt so selfish, as if in asserting her own interests she was neglecting her family's needs.

She put her tired feet on the ottoman and switched on the radio. Using the techniques she'd learned in yoga class, Jenny systematically relaxed her body, hoping that no one would find and disturb her.

Bea came in to say good-bye. "I'm going now, Jenny," she announced. "Is there anything else I can do for you?"

Jenny gave a sheepish grin over having weakened in her weaning attempts. "I was lazy," she admitted.

Bea shrugged. "A mother's got to do what she's got to do."

Jenny smiled at her friend's acceptance. "Go home," she told her. "You've already done too much. Take your envelope," she instructed, pointing to a small round table covered with a floor-length embroidered silk cloth trimmed with fringe that reached the floor. It was an antique from Spain.

There was an extra fifteen dollars for the day. Before Bea could put up a fight, Jenny stopped her with the hand that never failed to squelch rebuttals. "You deserve it, Bea. I was out all afternoon, and I'm still beat. How come you're still standing? Have you got a broom tied to your spine?"

Beatrice turned around to wag her full behind in Jenny's direction, giving testimony that she was untethered. "No use giving me this extra money, Jenny. My old man will just take it and waste it on something bad."

For a few minutes they discussed Bea's husband. He was a hard man whose problems went beyond the power of the balm of a good wife and two fine grown children to help.

"I'm not taking this money, Jenny Heath," Bea concluded. "You know the old proverb: give a man enough rope and he'll skip."

Jenny laughed in spite of herself. No, she'd never heard that one before. But she refused to take the money back.

Later, when Joyce and Karen and Matthew came home,

Jenny put the three of them to work taking the frozen whole wheat pizza crusts and the three quarts of homemade sauce out of the refrigerator, draining and cutting up the tofu soybean curd, and crushing the dried herbs that hung in bunches from the pantry ceiling.

Jenny put the baby into his crib before she preheated the oven and chopped fresh vegetables for the salad. She garnished the pizzas, put them in to bake, and ran upstairs to check on Amy, returning in a moment.

When Mister came through the door, he immediately chipped in to help Matthew pull a large platter out of a high cabinet. He went around making contact with the three helpers in the kitchen, and then signaled for Jenny to follow him out of the room.

"What is it?" Jenny asked, capping the bottle of penicillin that had been prescribed for Amy. But before she could get anything out of her husband, he had her in his strong arms, tasting her surprised but responsive lips. He took the medicine from her and placed it on the embroidered tablecloth behind him. His sweet mouth took her breath away as it pressed into her full lips. He ran his hands up her tired spine, eliciting a groan of pleasure from her. His hands lingered on her shoulders as he massaged deeply into her weariness.

"To what do I owe this glorious attention?" Jenny asked, her words slurred with wanting him.

"You didn't kiss me when you took off after lunch," Mister accused, pulling her pliant body more firmly against his own.

Jenny chuckled. "I ought to be stingy more often," she whispered, her voice a throaty growl.

"Is dinner far enough along to let the kids do the rest alone?" Mister asked, pulling back so she could see the sexy mischief in his eyes.

A smile lifted Jenny's lips as she considered Mister's intentions. He was such a thoughtful husband! He knew how important it was to her to have her routine broken. The rendezvous last night, the lunch today, and now this late-

The Family Plan

afternoon passion. "Oh, Mister," she purred, "do we dare?"

"Are you hungry?" he asked, nibbling on her chin.

"Not for food," she answered.

"Then why sit at the table?" he said reasonably.

Jenny returned to the kitchen to make some final arrangements. "Your father and I are going to take a nap. If anyone calls on the phone, take a message."

"A *nap!*" Karen exclaimed. "Why would anyone take a nap if they didn't *have* to?"

"Just do as your mother says," Mister instructed. "And afterward, clear the table."

"It's Matthew's turn to load the dishwasher," Joyce noted with satisfaction.

Jenny nodded in agreement.

"Where's Todd?" Karen wanted to know. She had a special affection for her older brother, who always responded to her shyness with a protective cloak of understanding.

Jenny and Mister smiled at each other, silently guessing the whereabouts of their dashing son. "I doubt he'll have an appetite—" Jenny began.

"For food," Mister finished.

"As soon as he comes in, please have him knock on our door," Jenny instructed.

"But I thought you were going to be napping," Joyce protested.

Mister put a persuasive arm around Jenny's shoulders.

"This isn't going to work," she mumbled as he led her away.

Mister's hand was massaging her muscles. "Just play it easy," he instructed. "C'mon."

A devilishly good feeling coursed through her body. Here she was, at dinnertime, about to disappear with her husband into the private world of their bedroom. She quickened her steps on the carpeted stairs.

From the kitchen she heard the usual din of conversation from her children, eliminating any doubts she'd harbored about the interlude. The children would be fine. They'd get along without her. They'd carry on as usual—maybe even be thankful for a dinner without parental supervision.

It made Jenny feel good that she could trust her family so completely. She and Mister had done a fine job of raising them with wholesome values.

"What are you thinking?" Mister asked as he locked the door to the master bedroom suite, which was decorated with swag curtains, heavy European tapestries, and massive antique furniture. It was a boudoir, a small recreation of palatial delights. And very insulated, very quiet.

"Just that you're the best father in the world," Jenny remarked as Mister's hands shamelessly molded her breasts in a seductive massage.

"And how do I rate as a husband?" Mister asked.

Jenny smiled, her eyes misting with passion and love. "Even better than that," she told him. "Mister, you're the best husband in this world and any other, and that includes Venus, the planet of love."

His strong, clean hands flicked open the top button of Jenny's tunic. His touch never failed to excite her, to fill her with pleasurable anticipation. This one simple gesture, executed with mastery and confidence, already had her aching for more. His practiced fingers undid another button, making her thrill with desire as her deep breaths lifted her breasts toward Mister.

"Do you ever wish you'd made love to another man, Jenny?" he asked. It was a familiar question, one Mister often used to begin a lively and heated reverie of shared fantasies that were an integral part of their lovemaking.

"Yes," she answered as her husband's slow hands popped open one button after the other.

"Tell me about it," Mister said as he turned on the pink nightlight and doused the glare from the ornate rococo ceiling fixture. "Tell me all about it."

3

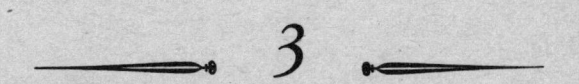

"I CAN'T DO THAT," Jenny protested, using the toe of one shoe to flick at the heel of the other and leaning back onto the sumptuous teal-blue bedspread Mister had brought her from Italy. "You'd be very disappointed," she added, dangling the shoe from her toe and smiling tauntingly at her husband.

Mister had the look of a man in no hurry to extricate secrets from his willing victim. His gray eyes looked so sexy and deep in the soft glow of the nightlight. He removed his jacket languidly as he stared down at his half-reclining wife. His eyes traveled from her abundant blond hair, over her face, and past the shadowy terrain he'd begun to uncover with his probing fingers. When his gaze reached her hips, it shifted up to her eyes and then once again traveled the distance to her crossed legs and the dangling shoe.

Bubbling anticipation effervesced in Jenny's breast. Her next breath was one she had to go after in the recesses of her lungs. Her eyes met Mister's in a seductive, smiling challenge. The look Mister returned gave her a sweet shiver of desire.

Already, with just their subtle glances and joking words, the couple was excited by the prospect of finally making love to each other. It was a common feeling for Jenny, this tingle of fun during foreplay. It was emblematic of their marriage. When they made love, it was always with a profound sense of belonging to one another—of giving up to each other the precious nectars and sighs and love sounds of desire. There were no problems, no inhibitions, no regrets.

Jenny watched Mister's every move as he began unbuttoning his shirt. She smiled at his able hand, knowing that soon its gentle and persuasive touch would be on her. She loved watching Mister's clothes fall away from his wonderful body.

As a smooth shoulder emerged from its hiding place inside his pastel shirt, Jenny was surprised by the effect it had on her. A flash of memory—played a thousand times—whisked past her mind's eye, touching off a sensory response in her womanly depths. There were times when, in Mister's arms, she'd clutch that shoulder and hold on for dear life; there were times she pressed her cheek against it and pushed her body more deeply against his; there were times, especially when the house was very, very quiet, that she bit hard into that shoulder in an effort to subdue her piercing cries during the tremendous rush of satisfaction Mister never failed to give her.

His hands now slowly pulled the shirttails from his belted slacks. With the next move, his shirt was off, and he was leaning over his adoring wife. His hands resting on either side of her body, he brought his lips slowly down to encounter hers.

She returned his gentle kiss with a slow and searching one of her own. A light moan rose in her throat and ended as a sigh on her lips. Mister fit his sweet mouth fully over hers and pulled her arm out from under her so that she collapsed beneath him into the luxurious tufts of the bedspread.

His hand squeezed hers as their kisses deepened. Jenny

The Family Plan

turned her palm in Mister's hand so that it was facing him, and their sensitive, tingly hands did a slow, erotic dance in each other's clutch.

Her other hand slid up along Mister's back and then made the trip in the opposite direction. She reveled in the gorgeous smoothness of his manly skin; she kneaded the muscles of his shoulders. Her loving hand dipped into the cleft of his strong spine and played its attentive tune on the sensuously undulating vertebrae.

"Oh," Mister moaned into her open mouth, "that feels so good!" He moved an inch back from her face and looked into her eyes. "How do you do that?" he asked.

She smiled at him and winked. "It's called touching," she teased.

Mister kissed her again. "Is that all it is?" he asked. "Touching?"

"Mmm," Jenny responded, her lips too busy kissing him to want to answer.

"Then touch me some more," Mister growled softly. He reached behind and took her arm. His hand traveled its length until he had a gentle but firm grip on her roving hand.

Again Jenny's breath quickened. She loved it when Mister directed her hand like this. She kissed him fervently as one part of her waited to see where he'd place her hand. He brought it to his mouth. He turned from her lips to lavish her palm with sweet, exciting kisses. He licked the sensitized skin until she thought she'd scream out in need. Taking his time, he bit gently into the ridge between her pinky and wrist, making her feminine soul open with desire.

And Jenny knew he was watching her every response. Watching her chest, still half-covered by her tunic, rise and fall with the passion. Watching her mouth fall lax and panting as the excruciating pleasure further softened her, making her a slave to his attentions. He opened her hand over his face and nibbled at the very center of her palm; then his slow tongue, ever eager to please, traveled to the junctions where her fingers met her palm. He took each of her digits into his mouth and sucked on them long and lovingly.

Jenny had no more will; she had no sense of anything other than her husband's patient, attentive caresses. For a split second she felt tears burning behind her eyes as she realized that good lovemaking was a mystical experience. It performed the highest goal of any spiritual endeavor, by bringing the lovers out of themselves, out of their egos, out of their selfishness, and into the realm of bliss, where they could experience the freedom and beauty of belonging not only to each other, but to the entire universe.

"Oh, Mister," she panted into her husband's shoulder. "I love you! I love you so much!" And the tears began to fall.

Mister smiled at Jenny and kissed away her streaming tears. He understood her, she knew. They had often talked about this wondrous ecstasy their lovemaking brought them. And when the children had been born, from Todd through baby Lloyd, Mister too had cried over the awe and miracle of it all.

Now he gave Jenny a soul kiss that embodied all his masculine need. His warm hands flicked her tunic from her shoulders. It fell lower, trapping her upper arms and immobilizing her. She chuckled as Mister's look assured her he wouldn't release the tunic's hold. With a mischievous glint in his eyes, he kissed her under the chin. His lips lingered there, tasting her softly, and Jenny threw her head back to give him better access. Then his mouth, like a waiting, taut, anxious animal of prey, blazed a slightly moist trail down into the valley between her breasts. His breath on her skin was a steamy sauna, a gentle catalyst opening her to its persuasive nudgings.

"Oh, Mister!" she breathed, half in dismay, as his lips just missed touching her nipples. He wouldn't touch them, she knew. And that knowledge both infuriated and inflamed her. For even though she was subject to wanton failures of caution, Mister was ever-mindful, ever-considerate of his wife's condition. Now, as she was trying so hard to wean the baby, Mister would not touch her breasts. "I might start nursing him more," she coaxed, half teasing her husband,

The Family Plan   41

who was always the more sensible one.

Mister looked up at her from between the soft mounds of her breasts. He shook his head but didn't utter a word. *Might* wasn't good enough, Jenny knew. What if she changed her mind about nursing? What if tomorrow she decided, as she had vehemently decided at least three times in the past two weeks, to end it once and for all? No, Mister would not stimulate her breasts when she was so unsure about continuing to nurse the baby. If she wanted to increase her flow, he'd leave that to her. As in their policies toward child-rearing, Mister felt obligated and responsible to give everyone he loved a fair chance—the chance to fail or succeed with decisions individually made.

Jenny smiled and shook her head. That Mister! So responsible, so thoughtful. She hated it sometimes! She wished he'd do to her breasts what she knew he could—what he did to them between children, at the times when he considered them objects of desire.

But Mister was nothing if not imaginative, and he showed that trait now as his lips slid to the hollow where her ribs formed a delta below her breasts. He buried his face in her softness and let his lips trail down to the slight, heaving mound of her stomach. Jenny heard his sigh of pleasure as his cheek rubbed along the swelling curve. She felt the rage of his passion as his lips met her hipbones, and she experienced the wave of love that told his lips and teeth just how to touch her and where.

Like a lazy animal enjoying his spoils, Mister nibbled at Jenny's hips, his head following the thrusting rhythm of her movements.

It was too much for Jenny. She needed to repay the attentions, to participate more fully. She yanked her right arm out of the tunic, but Mister was immediately on her, kissing her and trying to keep her from doing more than she was.

"You're crazy," she whispered to her husband. "I want to touch you."

Mister smiled. "How much?" he taunted.

"This much," Jenny responded as her free hand grabbed the back of Mister's strong neck and glued his lips to her mouth.

"How much?" he asked again.

"You'd better be quiet, Mister," she warned, "or you'll be in for real trouble."

"Trouble's never scared me off yet," Mister playfully reminded her.

Jenny could feel the glint glowing in her eyes. She worked her other hand out of her tunic. Mister stopped his kissing to help her get it off. Silently, they unbuckled Mister's eelskin belt and unbuttoned the mother-of-pearl button on his European slacks. Their hands worked together, touching provocatively as they freed his body. With one swift, tender motion, Jenny lowered Mister's pants to below his buttocks. He gently kicked the trousers off until they were lying in a heap at the foot of the bed.

Jenny so loved her Mister! The sight of his body gave her a rush of sensual desire mingled with a deep sense of caring. By usual standards, Mister was not the most handsome man in the world. His legs were slight, and his chest had only a small smattering of light hair on it, but to Jenny he was the most desirable and sexy lover anyone could ask for.

Mister fit his gentle hands into the waistband of Jenny's slacks and brought them off with a slow, lascivious move.

Now, both naked in the pink glow of their opulent bedroom, Jenny and Mister clung together. They touched each other everywhere, reveling in the feel of hot, smooth skin on skin. They soaked up the joy of their mutual, intense sense of nurturing. They relived the passion that sustained not only their marriage but their very lives. Tumbling over each other, they kissed deeply and wrapped their bodies around each other—Jenny's legs around Mister's buttocks, Mister's arms completely enfolding her torso. Their deep kisses sent them swimming in the familiar waters of each other's wants and needs.

Oh, how could she have ever wished for anything more

from life? How could she have wanted more excitement, more pleasure, more love than her wonderful husband so freely gave her?

"Tell me what you're thinking," Mister encouraged.

She tittered nervously and then told him. "You're my secret lover." She kissed him, crushing their lips together in urgent need. Mister's hands were molding themselves to her hips, to her waist, to the sides of her breasts that were pressed up against his chest. "No one knows we meet like this," she continued, shifting her consciousness to the fantasy where her lover was doing to her all the things Mister was doing. "And you can't stay long."

"Oh, then we'll have to hurry, won't we?" Mister teased.

"Oh, no!" Jenny countered. "What I mean is we can't stop for tea and biscuits after we've made love."

"Tea and biscuits?" Mister exclaimed, a loud, spontaneous laugh ejected from his throat. He chuckled at his wife's sense of humor as he shook his head lovingly at her.

Jenny ran a hand along her husband's side and wheedled it into the space between their stomachs. For long, seething moments the couple plied each other with their hands, intoxicating each other with their mastery. Each knew every inch, every curve, every crevice of the other's steamy body. Jenny felt light-headed and dizzy as she concentrated only on the sensations she and Mister were brewing. She pressed her legs into Mister's buttocks to keep him closer still. "Now," she whispered into his strong shoulder.

"Uh-uh," he refused, obviously too engrossed to utter a word.

Jenny sought to make him see things her way. She pressed herself tightly to his body, but found that he took advantage of the situation to roll her on top of him. He pushed on her legs until her full length was upon his and she nestled into the nook his legs made. Her lips nibbled at Mister's chin, they slinked down to his chest, where she tasted his sweet flesh and enjoyed the hard strain of muscles under his excited nipples. She kissed his taut stomach and his narrow hips. Then her lips fell to nuzzling him in a heated, wanton frenzy.

Mister groaned and pulled her up so that he could kiss her lips. He started to say something but then let out a muffled moan that twisted his full, sexy mouth into a grimace of pleasure. His eyes closed as if he were in pain, but instantly opened to give his wife an incredulous look. Suddenly shy over the pleasure she'd given her husband, Jenny let out a tiny giggle and hid her face in his shoulder. But her own sense of adventure and Mister's persuasive hands soon brought her out.

"We have to be very quiet," she said, picking up her fantasy once more. "If they come to the door, hide under the sheets," she advised.

"Gladly," Mister answered. "As long as you're under them."

"Okay." Jenny agreed, now wishing that "they" would make an appearance in her fantasy. "They might not recognize you anyway," she murmured, afraid that with Mister's continued probings she would not be able to finish her story.

"What do I look like?" Mister whispered as his hands dipped between Jenny's thighs and made her let out a purr of delight.

"You're fair-skinned, with dirty-blond hair..." She trailed off as her senses became overwhelmed by Mister's insistent and animated fingers.

"Go on," Mister encouraged.

"You're about thirty-nine, you're in interesting work..." She had to stop; her breath was coming in short, deep gasps that ended in tiny moans of pleasure.

"What does your fantasy lover do?" Mister asked.

It was exciting to have to think of something else while Mister's hands were working magic with her senses. It was like being brought to exhilarating heights over and over again, making the final ascent that much sweeter and poignant. But now she wished she'd never started this little reverie; she wanted only to surrender to Mister's hot, piercing probings. "He pretends to come sell me brushes," she said, half choking on a suppressed laugh. "Then he locks the door and makes love to me."

The Family Plan 45

"Ah! A brush salesman, eh?" Mister approved as he lifted Jenny's hips so that she was sitting astride him.

For a moment their eyes met, and Jenny whispered, "Please, Mister, I feel like you've dug a deep trench in me, and only you can fill it."

Mister smiled and kissed her, bringing her lips down to his. At the same time, he slid her body down and over his so that she was filled with his manliness. She released a gasp into his mouth. No matter how many times they'd made love, the first second was always a beautiful surprise.

"Shall I call in the salesman?" Mister asked as his hips set a slow, penetrating rhythm.

Jenny couldn't talk. The part of her brain that regulated speech was beyond her control. The only thing she could do was make the love sounds that came out of her of their own accord. Mister's mouth was fitted over hers, and he returned her tender moans with his own urgent panting. His tongue slid along hers and then tickled the roof of her mouth until that, too, burned with the frenzy of their lovemaking. The deeper his tongue probed, the closer he brought her to ecstasy with his masterful body and hands. Jenny was running her palms over his skin, feeling his every muscle. Mister had his hands between their stomachs, providing the additional ministrations that would make their lovemaking complete for her.

"You're my secret lover, too," Mister told Jenny as her senses spun with concentrating on only one thing. "And you're all alone when I pay a call to sell you a brush."

Despite their intent lovemaking, both of them laughed. Jenny had a sudden vision of Mister appearing at her door, brushes in hand and passion on his face. She threw her head back, releasing a throaty, deep chuckle that emanated from the vibrant depths Mister was sharing.

He held her tightly and turned their moist bodies over so that he was looking down into her face. Jenny smiled back at him and closed her eyes in profound satisfaction. Oh, yes. He was her Mister, her man, her life's mate.

"What am I wearing?" Jenny managed as she again flowed with Mister's intention to keep bringing them high, then low, then higher still, until, she knew, they'd both tug each other up to the loftiest peak.

"You're in an Oriental kimono, an Imperial robe with a five-clawed eagle spread across the back..."

Jenny's chuckle interrupted Mister's reverie. Her taut breasts bounced beneath him. He must have already realized that she was laughing because he was bringing his profession into bed; he gave her an exaggerated look of indignation and then placed his full weight on her, kissing her lips with a sweet and tender poignancy. "I love you, darling," he whispered when his lips turned toward her cheek. The lips so close yet not fully touching her ear made Jenny shudder with desire. She let out an excited moan when he enveloped it in the soft, wet cavern of his mouth.

Whispering now and energetically stimulating her where they merged, Mister brought Jenny up for what she knew was the final climb. In the part of her body that seemed made of ether, the part that somehow lived both inside and outside of her, a pit gaped open. Jenny could almost see into the swirling, bottomless hole shrouded in a brilliant white mist. Mister was whispering frantically now. "You don't like the things I show you, so I take out my *pièce de résistance*—a hairbrush for your silky, long hair."

Jenny was past recognizing words. She was biting hard into Mister's right shoulder, trying to muffle the heated animal sounds that escaped her straining throat. "Your kimono slips open, and I see your delicate breasts," Mister was saying, the difficulty of his words betraying the fact that he, too, was almost beyond them. "Your hair's so lustrous, so soft, so perfect..."

Jenny nuzzled her hips closer to her husband's, like a hungry creature seeking nourishment. "Mister!" she panted softly, her throat constricted with unreleased and surging passion. "Mister! Here it is..."

"Your hair so soft, so sexy, so shiny-black," Mister was saying as he, too, was completely taken with the moment. Another movement, another groping, straining motion, and both of them were shoved—like stones in a catapult, like

The Family Plan 47

pellets in a sling—over the last obstacle and onto the peak of springy, grassy moss, where they basked in the sunshine of their love.

Jenny was immediately seized with little staccato laughs that shook her breathless, spent body. She was in the rarest of moods—the most relaxed and relieved good humor possible.

Mister lay across her, tenderly stroking the side of her left breast, which was crushed beneath him. He peeked at her and then laughed too. His eyes closed for a second. "You're quite a beautiful woman," he murmured, an inexplicable sadness coloring his words.

"Hey," Jenny teased, *"My* hair isn't black and lustrous!" She grabbed a pillow and let it land on Mister's backside. Then she laughed more and hugged her wonderful husband to herself. "See how unexciting I've become?" she whispered into his ear. "Even my fantasy lover looks like my own husband!"

She cleared her throat and settled in deeper under Mister's quiet body, exclaiming, "I'd better do something about this problem before I get swallowed up by drudgery. Imagine! There'll come a time when the kids are grown, and you're away on a trip, and I won't have anything to do." She pulled a stray lock of hair from her mouth and took a deep, satisfying breath. "I mean I won't know *how* to do anything. Did you know that they're starting Matthew on a computerized study system? He'll be a technocrat by the age of eight, and I'll still be making a wide arch as I walk past the microwaves in Sears. You know, I really believe those things are lethal. That eventually everyone who's ever had a rubbery egg from one will mutate into a separate species..." She noticed how limp and quiet her husband was, remembering that most times after making love they rested serenely in each other's arms or slept.

She smiled and pulled the covers up over his body. "Sorry, Mister," she whispered. "Going off and chattering like that— I must sound like a scratched record." She kissed the top of his head. "Sleep," she whispered softly. "I'll go check on the kids—or what's left of them..." She hitched her body up to pull away from Mister.

But his hold on her tightened, preventing her from moving further. Her first reaction was to rebel; once she had her mind set on "checking the kids," it was usually impossible for Mister to stop her. But there was something urgent in her husband's embrace, so she slinked back into it, completely immersing her body in the heat of his. She adjusted the covers so that they trapped the steaminess their lovemaking had created.

As she waited for him to speak, she listened to her husband's breathing. It was still unsettled, as though he were spacing his breaths until his thoughts ripened.

Suddenly reality took a tailspin as fear gripped Jenny's heart. She smoothed Mister's damp hair off his forehead and whispered, "What's wrong, darling?" She panicked at his silence. "Are you tired of hearing me complain?" Hugging him close, she let out a tiny, frightened chuckle. "Tell me. Please, Mister. Please talk to me."

When Jenny saw Mister's anguished expression, a terrible, icy dread swept over her. She felt utterly disoriented by his uncharacteristic stare. "What?" she whispered, fearing the word would choke her.

Mister closed his eyes for an instant and then opened their pained gray depths to her. "I don't know where to start," he said. "I just..." He sighed and leaned his head onto Jenny's breasts, burrowing his cheek into them.

"It's all right, darling," Jenny hastened to assure him. "I told you today—we've weathered so much. We can—"

"I wasn't thinking of you just now as we made love," Mister whispered, his eyes sincere and worried.

Jenny let out a breathy laugh, like that of a swimmer emerging from icy depths to greet the sun-splattered surface. "Is that what's eating at you, you dunce?" she exclaimed. "That's what fantasy is! That's what I complain I can't do—get out of my own little world enough to..."

Mister was shaking his head. There would be no arguing with the man when he looked like this. "No," he confessed.

The Family Plan

"It was more than just a harmless fantasy." He looked into his wife's eyes, and she knew he was seeing the trust and love fostered by their years spent together.

Jenny let slip all her defenses and judgments. She opened her sight and heart to whatever her beloved, devoted Mister had to share. She secretly made light of his confession that he'd been thinking of another woman; all lovers created elaborate fantasies. It was simply a matter of Mister's not being accustomed to the practice. He was such a dear, good, and faithful man.

She could tell that he'd recognized the sincerity in her eyes, but she didn't get the usual open and relieved response from him. Instead, he looked away, obviously disappointed with himself. Was he even a little flustered and frustrated that Jenny was being so understanding?

Among the myriad emotions that sprang up in her, Jenny suddenly felt defiance rear its head. No, she wouldn't make this any easier for him now that Mister was acting like a stranger. She wouldn't make it easier by being cruel or defensive. She'd weather whatever he had to say and remain her good-natured self. "I'm listening very carefully, darling," she told her husband. "Go on."

Mister rolled off her, taking care not to pull the blanket from her. Jenny readjusted the quilt and propped herself on one elbow to watch as Mister stared blankly at the ceiling. "You don't deserve this, Jenny," he preambled the coming speech.

"Probably not," she agreed.

"You've never given me reason to feel dissatisfied with you. You're the best wife in the world." He rolled onto his elbow so that he was facing her. His hand reached out to stroke her upper arm. "And the best mother—"

"Mister!" she whispered. "It can't be! You're not having an affair, are you?"

To his sad smile of denial, Jenny grabbed his face in her hands and shook his head. "So tell me what's wrong!"

He smiled wryly and sighed. "All the time you've been going through a crisis, wondering what you've missed by being my wife, fantasizing about life outside our relationship, being frustrated that the kids bring so many overwhelming responsibilities, I guess I've been having a crisis of my own."

It didn't come as a complete surprise. In fact, part of her felt something akin to relief at his confession. Though she wouldn't have consciously acknowledged that Mister seemed to be experiencing some kind of mid-life crisis, she must have been suspecting it all along. In fact, in voicing her own complaints, she had perhaps been attempting to get Mister to express his!

If there was one thing the two of them possessed, it was an infallible sensitivity to each other. The only reason Jenny hadn't had a grip on the monster that had been gnawing at Mister was because he himself hadn't realized its presence until now—not even during, but *after* the act of lovemaking.

Jenny put a shaky hand to her moist forehead and let out a jittery laugh of relief. "Oh, Mister, I'm so glad!"

He shook his head again and touched her upper arm in an uncharacteristically feeble show of affection. The slight touch affected Jenny more than any words he could have uttered. It sobered her, sending her tailspinning into the netherworld of doubt and fear.

"Jenny," Mister exclaimed, taking her limp and shocked body into his arms and covering her face with poignant kisses that tasted of farewells at railway stations during a war. "I have no right. No right. But I can't help it. I didn't even know it. I swear I didn't. But now—I can't express why yet—I feel so...lost, so alone, so..."

Jenny lay passively in her husband's arms. No tears came. "Empty!" she offered.

"Yes," Mister admitted. "As though a ghost that had been haunting me finally made me vacate my body."

"And now this 'ghost' has possession?" Jenny asked, knowing full well the terrible feeling her husband was describing. Hadn't she been experiencing the very same sense of not knowing who she was and what she was about? A silent and very hot tear finally crept down her fevered cheek.

The Family Plan

Mister squeezed her to him, pressing against her with all his might. But she felt no pain, no stirring. She was too hurt and bewildered.

"Oh, Mister," she whispered as she cried into her husband's neck. "But do you still love me? For me, that was the one thing that helped. I love you and the children more than life itself!" Her voice cracked. "Do you still love us? Do you love *me?*"

"Yes, Jenny, of course I do. I'd have to be dead not to feel my love for you and the children." He absently rubbed his clean-shaven cheek against Jenny's hair, the pressure tingling her scalp. "But I'm afraid, Jenny," he confessed, saying it with inordinate pain. "I don't know what will become of me, and I have a very, very frightening thing to tell you."

His grip on Jenny tightened until she could hardly breathe, hardly hear, hardly think. "You remember our conversation with Heddy today?" Jenny barely heard another word. Heddy Lock. *Heddy Lock!* Long, straight lustrous black hair. No! It couldn't be that Mister was in love with her!

4

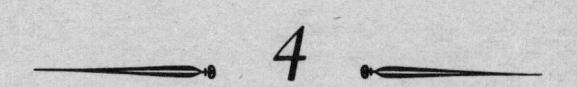

"WHEN SHE WAS talking about her marriages," Mister's far-off voice was saying, as though from a still-lingering nightmare, "I felt I wanted to—I'm not really sure—protect her, I suppose. I've come to know her quite well, and I just get the feeling that she's not living up to her potential as a woman. That she hasn't had the opportunity to really blossom..."

Jenny's heart was bursting with grief at Mister's words. She was both desperate and terrified to know his innermost feelings toward the woman. "Maybe she's happy with the person she is at this point in her life," she challenged. She shot up out of bed and threw her satin robe over her nakedness. The tears were streaming down in a terrible torrent.

"Jenny, please, just let me talk a minute. I just have to figure this out aloud. We've always shared our pains—"

"How dare you!" she cried, not knowing how to exorcise the pacing, ranting tigress in her. "How dare you take the sanctity of what we have together and use it to hurt me!" She yanked the belt of her robe so tightly that she could hear some stitches rip. "Don't treat me like your best friend!" she pleaded, her fists two balled and painful wads, two ineffectual, cramped appendages.

She turned her tortured face toward Mister's. "I love you," she explained. "I *love* you. I'm unhappy with the rut I'm in, but, Mister, I still *love* you! Don't pal up to me and pretend we're experiencing the same pain!" She could hardly talk. Her tongue thick with hurt.

Mister was up and trying to touch her, to draw her close. "Please, Jenny, calm down. Let's talk."

"Talk?" she screamed incredulously. "You have no idea of what you've done to me! You don't understand, Mister— *my* complaint isn't with *you!* Oh, I know I carry on a lot and I make a lot of jokes about it, but don't you see? You're still safe—you have me to adore and love you."

"I love you, too," Mister asserted, finally succeeding in grabbing her upper arms and shaking her so that she'd focus her attention on him.

"Stop it," she warned, vainly tugging her arms. "If you don't love me anymore, then let's be adult about it. Go to your precious Heddy!"

As soon as she said it, she realized that she actually harbored no malice toward the innocent woman. It wasn't in Jenny's nature to be spiteful.

Mister shook Jenny again, and she took a labored, deep, and broken breath. "Okay," Mister soothed, "let's be adult about it. The first step is hearing me out." He sent his plaintive gray gaze into her eyes, then gave a faint and tender smile. "Can we talk?" he asked, his face so familiar, so dear, so beloved.

Jenny fell against his chest and sobbed into it. She tried to speak, but nothing came. Finally she nodded.

Mister led her to the bed and sat her on its edge. He knelt before her, his head in her lap, waiting for her to stop crying. After a few moments, Jenny shoved his head away. "That's better," Mister stated as he regained his balance. "Knock this square peg I call a head off."

"I ought to blacken your other eye," Jenny warned.

Mister resumed his position at her feet and asked, "May I?" about putting his head down again.

"At your own risk," Jenny assured him, already feeling more willing to talk things through with her husband.

"I never said I was in love with Heddy," he began. Playfully, he raised his head and pretended to dodge a punch.

"Oh stop it, you dope," she chided, still infuriated, but softening toward him as her tremendous feelings of love resurfaced and her trust in his love for her was reborn. "When you get it, it'll be without warning," she promised, showing a fist.

Mister opened the fist to kiss it. He looked from her palms to her eyes as the angry red marks of her clenched fingers were revealed. "Oh, Jenny. My sweet, dear Jenny," he lamented, placing a soft kiss on each engraved crescent. He looked up at her. "I never intended to hurt you, my love. Please be patient with me. I'm just so confused at this point in my life."

"Are you in love with Heddy Lock?" was all Jenny could ask.

"I told you," he said softly. "No. But she brings out strange feelings in me."

"So? Ask her to leave Piper. We'll all be happier," Jenny retorted, knowing full well that such action would solve nothing.

"She reminds me of my former self, I guess," Mister offered as a possible explanation for the attraction. "And I suppose you might say she reminds me of things I might yet become." He lifted his eyes to Jenny. "I can't lie to you, Jenny. I do feel attracted to her. She's so vulnerable..."

Jenny smacked her forehead. "So now you're punishing me for being strong!" she exclaimed, her frustration causing her voice to rise a decibel.

"No, Jenny, I love it that you're strong, but I think maybe you don't need me like you once did, and—oh, I don't know what the hell I'm getting at, darling! I just feel that, well, at the risk of incurring your wrath, I still believe that

I feel the same thing that you do—a kind of emptiness, a sense of 'Well, what now?' a vastly terrifying doubt." His moist and sincere eyes beseeched her. "You do understand, don't you, my Jenny?"

"Mister, I don't understand anything right now. For a woman to complain about housework or kids—that's one thing. But to have my world and the course of our lives so completely threatened—it frightens me, Mister. What will become of us? Is there a pill to cure what we have? Is there a computer program to run through for the answers?"

"Jenny, it's our problem, and ours alone. Not yours alone or mine alone, or the children's—"

"Or Heddy's?" Jenny asked, hoping for the right answer.

"Or Heddy's," Mister conceded.

"But eventually, Mister, eventually, will you profess your feelings to her?"

"Lord, I hope not!" he answered.

At that, the rage and fear in Jenny reared their frightful heads. She freed herself of Mister's hold and began a frantic, aimless pacing that, no matter how fast, could not keep time with the desperate thoughts racing through her mind. "Wait a minute—hold the line," she murmured in an attempt to isolate at least one pertinent, revealing question to ask her husband. "Wait!" she cried, running a shaky hand through her tousled hair.

"Jenny, I'm so sorry. I never expected you to react this badly," Mister said, throwing the quilt around his shoulders and advancing toward his wife. "After all, you've been unhappy, too."

"Don't touch me," Jenny pleaded. "Don't." She put up both palms to stop his advance, but he kept coming. She turned from him, but he caught her arm and swung her around.

"Do you imagine you're the only one who wonders about things that might have been, Jenny?" he asked. But she wouldn't answer—she couldn't. The nature of what he was experiencing was so different! "I'm not saying I want to give up our lives together. I just needed to share my doubts

The Family Plan 57

with you, the way you and Heddy did at lunch today."

The person who espoused total honesty in a marriage ought to be whipped into stiff peaks, Jenny thought. Then she laughed at her own joke, realizing with ironic dread that she was doing it again: she'd used a common cookbook term about eggs to express her deepest feelings.

"What is it, darling?" Mister asked, his eyes concerned and startled. "What do you find funny in this?"

For a moment Jenny was tempted to feign insanity. She wanted to elicit that look of compassion from Mister again. Perhaps if he felt his wife's mind was at stake, he'd turn back the clock, undo the words, not feel his dissatisfaction, not be attracted to Heddy. But Jenny knew that would be not only absurd but cruel. She had never played games with her husband's emotions. She'd never used feminine guiles to manipulate him; she felt beyond such archaic and false techniques.

Her common sense and intelligence took the front line in this battle with the only man she'd ever loved, the only human being through whom she identified herself, the only one she'd trusted above all others with the custody of her very soul.

Her body relaxed in his arms, and she looked into his tortured eyes. For some odd reason she felt extremely attracted to Mister right now. A burning longing took up residence in her, and she wished above everything else to make love to Mister.

She hadn't felt this desperate burning in just this way for years. She suspected it was the result of feeling that he might no longer be hers, that they might never make love again in the way they always had—that she was losing something very dear and sweet and vital.

Mister was stroking her hair and making a soft, soothing sound.

She looked up at him, intent on being rational, but the overwhelming attraction she felt was nibbling seductively at her insides. She couldn't bear the beauty, the pain, the sincerity of his beloved face. His forehead was wrinkled in a deep, concerned crease; his gray eyes were soft with hurt, bewilderment, and an eagerness to calm her. Mister Heath. Lloyd Heath. Lloyd. She seldom called him that because of its meaning: gray, or dark. Often she'd felt it suited him because of the color of his eyes, but today the real meaning, the one she'd feared, seemed obvious. He was a murky, dark stranger—someone who lived in the shadows of daily life with a deep secret locked away.

"Wait, Mister," Jenny pleaded. "Explain it to me. Please. I want to understand! What happened? Why, all of a sudden, do you find yourself attracted to another woman?"

Mister shrugged. His eyebrows drew the skin over his nose into a handsome, mature frown. "I'm not sure, Jenny. She's not like other women. She's out in the world, facing the problems there. Yet she's very feminine and delicate. She seems unhappy—perhaps a little like you and me in that respect. I want to nurture her...but she wants to be independent and capable. And sometimes, when I see her handling clients or dealers on the phone, I feel there's something very sexy about her."

It was more than Jenny could take. Mister was describing the very woman she herself wanted to be. "Can't you see, Lloyd?" she pleaded. "It's so unfair of you to hold those traits in her favor and against me. You're penalizing me for not being the very thing you've kept me from being!"

"Do you mean that I've made you unhappy, Jenny?" he asked softly, looking into her face for the answer. "That I've made you into something you don't like?"

Jenny felt exasperated. "Yes," she answered. "Yes and no. I don't blame you..." She stared at him in suspense. "Do you blame *me?*" He shook his head. Slightly reassured, she continued, "It's just how things have gone. Listen, I've reviewed this a million times in my mind. We've built a situation step by step. Each phase seemed right and good at the time. Now that the product of all those steps is here, something inside us has changed."

"We're getting older," Mister offered softly. "And for the first time we sense that time will eventually run out on us."

The Family Plan

Jenny stared at the man who had so astutely put into words the something that had been eluding her. She stood on tiptoes and planted a moist kiss on his mouth. "Yes," she mused aloud. "Yes, you're absolutely right."

"But what happens to the children? The finances? The house? The very reality we've created?" Mister queried. "The material things can be done away with, but the responsibilities toward the others—our children, brought here by our own impulses—those won't dematerialize."

Jenny's eyes were filling with tears. "So you *have* been giving this some thought."

Mister hung his head and nodded. "Not consciously," he assured her. "I think I reached most of these conclusions from listening to you!" He set their trembling bodies rocking slightly.

The tears were already trickling down Jenny's neck and into her robe. The room, filled with the pink glow of their small light covered in frosted antique glass, looked so frivolous. She had once loved every piece of furniture and every picture on the walls. She'd once felt part and parcel of this house, its every creak and quirk. But suddenly she wasn't in love with it anymore.

Mister took his wife's chin in his hand and lifted her lips to his. As they kissed, she felt his excitement rising strong and hard between them, and it gave her inordinate joy. Oh yes, as long as she and Mister still had this need for each other, they'd be all right. It wasn't wholly sexual, although tonight it was manifesting itself in that way. It was almost purely emotional, for she knew he was feeling that same burning attraction she felt. That overpowering desperation to keep and hold on to what was theirs, to drink from each other all the nectar of love, the juices of desire, the poignant and absolutely mutual bond that tied them heart and soul.

She responded eagerly to Mister's desperate and passionate kisses. She wrapped her body around his—feet around calves, arms around torso—and let him carry her to the bed. He lay her on its edge and immediately blazed a wanton trail from her swollen lips to her heaving breasts to her feminine desire, where he lingered, intent and desirous, until she cried out in fulfillment. Then he eased his body onto hers and changed her gentle, passionate cooings into rhythmic sounds of sorrow and joy. And again he lifted her onto the grassy knoll of the final ascent. Again he shot them high and far. Again they were as one.

But this time it hadn't been the lovemaking of two happily married people enjoying what they always did, sure that they always would. It was different now. There had been a dense and overpowering sensation of loss; they'd made love like two people whose hourglass was running low. And just as their lovemaking before had been emblematic of their life before, this episode reflected the haunting dread they both felt; that time was running short, and that the very things they both desperately clung to were keeping them from exploring more distant horizons.

Jenny knew something had changed for them in this afternoon interlude. At breakneck speed, their lives were going to change. Something had to give soon, but for now, all Jenny wanted, and all Mister seemed to want, was the love and security they'd built over the last nineteen years.

"Mister, I'm scared," Jenny confessed into her husband's shoulder, that pillar of strength, that intimate friend.

"I feel the danger, too," Mister confided as he held his wife in a tender clutch.

"What'll happen to us?" she asked.

"I won't let anything happen that you don't know about," Mister assured her.

But Jenny began crying again. "Don't change, Mister, please don't change."

First he sighed, and then he kissed Jenny's parted, anguished lips. "I'll try, Jenny. I promise I'll try not to."

In a bright and clear recess of Jenny's mind, she knew that what her husband promised would be impossible. The nature of life was change. Still, she clung to his words, trying to let him know that she truly understood. "We've been lucky, you and I, Mister. Almost two decades, and we've grown together. How many marriages can make that claim?" She felt she had to be brave. A tortured smile tensed her lips as she wept against her Mister's body. "Haven't we?" she asked tearfully. "Everything changes, everything grows. I only pray that this time we make it together, like we have in the past." The wish came from the deepest, most sensitive part of her soul. It traveled through her constricted chest and into her strained throat. "I love you my darling Mister!" she exclaimed. "I love you with all my heart!"

They rose and showered solemnly, each one washing the other. The act that had always been executed with playful fervor was now completed in awed and marveling mystery—as though they'd just discovered they were strangers who'd been sharing a lifetime. They were intimate, and yet they were shy. Familiar, yet cautious.

Jenny was blow-drying her hair in the bathroom when Mister came to report that the only sounds he'd heard from the children when he'd stood at the head of the stairs were those of one of their favorite TV shows and of a lively board game the middle children were playing.

Jenny smiled in a form of relief, but somehow the information meant little to her. She lay the dryer down and wrapped her terry cloth bathrobe more snugly around her. Folding herself into Mister's waiting arms, she whispered something that had come to her, like a flash, only that instant. "You're the most important person in my life, Mister. The kids—they'll grow up and leave us. They'll mate as we did, and the only ones left will be me and you."

"Haven't you always known that, my darling?" Mister asked, lifting her chin to gaze into her eyes.

"I was supposed to, I guess, but it never registered. I never felt I had so much at stake as I do tonight. I took it for granted that you'd always be mine."

"I am yours, Jenny. Yours alone. Believe me. I'm entertaining some very odd ideas right now, but even in my personal quandary, my guiding force is my love for you. Don't be afraid that I'd ever do or say or even think one thing in which you haven't been considered."

"But, Mister, what if your dissatisfaction grows? What if you come to resent me or the children? What if, in a moment of doubt, I can't be there?"

"I told you," Mister whispered softly, "I'm just going through the same thing you are." He tapped her chin with his index finger. "I'd no sooner hurt you than you'd hurt me."

"But still, things will have to change for us. It won't go away on its own."

Mister held her tightly and sighed into the top of her head. "We're both feeling itchy. We both want change. And we've been lucky enough to be able to share that with each other." His lips nuzzled into her hair. "It's not as though we've fallen out of love," he reasoned. "It's just another adventure to have together, another chance for growth."

Jenny's insides quivered at the thought of her limited control in the matter. "I believe you, Mister. I trust you and know that you love me."

His eyes twinkled with gentle merriment. "So we're in agreement? We'll see each other through to the end?"

"To a new beginning," she corrected. "We both feel trapped, but at least we have each other. That's the ticket."

"No more crazy ideas of desertion?" he prodded.

Jenny took a few choppy breaths. A subtle realization struck her: another woman in this situation might feel even less secure. But because of the bonds of trust and love she and Mister had forged, she'd always felt a certain personal freedom in being his wife. He never manipulated her, never deliberately stifled her. In his nurturing embrace, she'd been able to grow through the years. "Why would you want to leave something so perfect?" she reasoned, poking him in a ticklish spot along his side.

"Precisely," he agreed. "It's not that we've failed; we're only experiencing growing pains."

Oh, relief! Their marriage was going to be its own cure. Jenny's head was pounding with the fears she'd just experienced, but at least there was hope. A lot of work ahead, but hope.

There was a light tap at the door. "What is it?" Mister called out, not breaking his protective hold on his wife.

"It's me, Pop. Todd."

Mister looked at Jenny. "When did this house acquire a Pop?" he queried. "I thought only Dads and Moms lived here."

"Pops are grown-up dads," Jenny reasoned, not expecting her eighteen-year-old son to run around calling "Daddy."

"Don't look so understanding," Mister warned. "Maybe Mommies grow up to be Mops."

"Oh, there are already too many of those in the utility room," Jenny quipped, relief at not having lost her sense of humor washing over her. She took a deep, liberating breath.

"What is it, Todd? Can it wait?" Mister called, throwing on his bathrobe just in case it couldn't.

"No, Pop, it's sort of an emergency. I sort of need some, well, advice, I guess."

Mister approached the door. "The prodigal son returns," he said into Todd's face as he let him into the bedroom.

Todd looked around in a kind of confusion. "Pink lights?" he questioned. "Do you guys burn incense, too?"

"Of course," Mister answered, settling into the armchair near the bed. "And we chant mantras, too."

Todd knew when he was being ribbed, and being a Heath, he knew how to dish it out, too. "Give my regards to the Dalai Lama when you're in China next month," he retorted.

"The Dalai Lama was usurped years ago, Todd, when his monastery was still in Tibet, and Tibet wasn't in China."

Jenny playfully pulled on Todd's ear. "You haven't come for one of your father's famous history lessons," she remarked.

Todd took his mother's hands and led her to sit on the needleworked bench at her vanity. "Why so sweaty, Ma?" he asked. Jenny and Mister exchanged knowing glances on her new title.

Todd paced a bit before speaking. "I have to tell you straight. I don't know any other way," he began. "You met Peggy today. Did you like her?"

"I'd have to examine her credentials more closely," Mister said, a friendly edge of sarcasm in his voice. Evidently Mister was getting the same sneaky feeling that Jenny was.

"Now, Todd," Jenny began, relinquishing the seat that she guessed was supposed to soften the blow, "the theory in sitting someone down before asking for advice is that it is supposed to shorten their distance to the floor after they faint," she said, staring at her firstborn son who, to her, was still a young boy.

"Then you know I want to marry her," Todd sighed, closing his beautiful gray eyes.

Jenny and Mister stared at each other. Even though they'd guessed what was coming, the news still hit like a punch in the stomach.

Jenny reached out for Todd's hand as her knees faltered. He laughed a tiny laugh as he sat her down again.

"Oh, wow! That was so easy!" Todd whooped. "You're the best parents in the world. I can't believe it—wait till I tell her!" He was flying high, Jenny could see.

"Hold it, son," Mister said, getting up and betraying his shock by his own uneasy footing. "When do you expect to marry? I mean, this isn't like deciding to try out for the debating team or something."

"I'm a senior this year," Todd answered, still clearly ecstatic over having been able to voice himself so effortlessly. "In June."

"June?" both parents echoed protestingly.

"What about college, Todd?" Mister reminded.

"You and Ma both went to college after you were married."

"Yes, but that was different," Jenny heard herself say. Lame! Lame! Lame! she admonished herself. She ought to say something perceptive—and quickly!

Mister put a hand on Todd's shoulder. "Don't expect your mother and me to approve of this irresponsible idea, son." As soon as the words were past his lips, Jenny could tell her husband was regretting them as she'd regretted hers. They were failing to communicate meaningfully.

She stood up and looked Todd directly in the eyes. "What

your father and I are trying to say is that even though we did marry young, and we did get our educations eventually, and we did raise six gorgeous, wonderful, loving..." It was too much for Jenny.

Mister sheltered her in his trembling arms and picked up where she left off. All he managed, unfortunately, was, "Your mother is right, Todd."

Todd was looking from one to the other in bewilderment. The emotion that most hurt Jenny was that of the disappointment fluttering through his eyes. "Right? Right about what?" Todd wanted to know. "And don't pull any of this we-want-life-to-be-better-for-you garbage!" he snapped. "I thought you two were the kind of parents who were beyond that lame line."

The thought that rang through Jenny's mind as she watched Todd in this uncharacteristic anger was that he really was in love with Peggy. The realization brought back a flood of memories of the time she and Mister had decided, against considerable disapproval and adverse conditions, to marry. She recalled how they'd cried in each other's arms, the desperation of what they felt drawing them even closer. She looked at her adamant child, and her heart went out to him. Nothing would stop him. He was really in love.

"We probably understand what you're feeling a lot better than you imagine, Todd," Jenny said as she put her trembling palm on his tense and vibrating back. He felt so young, so tender, so vulnerable to her.

"Then why are you both pulling this routine?" he retorted. "You got married young. You had kids young. You went to school. Shee-it!" he exclaimed in frustration. "And you two have got more going between you than any of my friends' parents."

"Todd," Mister put in with a gentle, understanding tone to his authoritative voice. Jenny could feel her son tensing under its effect. "You're more intelligent than that. You can't simply say that because your mother and I are happy, you and Peggy necessarily will be."

Todd took an exasperated breath that lifted his lean back

under Jenny's hand. "You don't understand," he accused, using the phrase that could hurt his parents more than any other. "Of course I'm more intelligent than that. What I'm really mad about is your hypocritical attitude! After all, just because you *say* it might be different for us doesn't mean it has to be. You and Mommy succeeded. Why don't you cut me and Peggy some slack!"

At the sound of the endearment Todd had called her all her life, Jenny's tears streamed silently down her face. She wasn't crying about losing a son. She was crying over his innocence. If the truth were made known, Todd would discover that at this very moment in his parents' lives they were in the most frightening position ever—that the relationship he so admired was in peril, that Jenny and Mister were both dissatisfied with the life they'd wrought, that they both wanted another chance, they had both missed out on something by creating what they had as early as they had.

She and Mister now felt that those decisions they made nineteen years ago might as well have been chiseled into granite. If they acted on their frustrations, they'd be destroying not only each other, but their children, and everything they had ever worked for. Jenny was aware that many marriages had to go through similar crises, and she also knew that few endured intact. If it weren't for the profound love she and Mister shared, they wouldn't stand a chance against this test. She wanted to warn her son of the dangers, express the extraordinary devotion marriage involved.

"Todd," Jenny pleaded, "Can't this decision wait? Your father and I—"

"It can't wait, Ma, because Peggy needs me now. I can't put her on hold." He sat down on the bed and looked into his long-boned, fine hands that so resembled his father's. "You see, the reason I never brought her home was because she's married."

He held out his hands and leaned backward. "Wait," he instructed before either of his parents could react. "She's getting an annulment. It's finally coming through this month. It's been eight months, and they haven't consummated the marriage."

The Family Plan 67

Mister narrowed his eyes in concern. "You're sure of that?"

Todd slammed his fists into his sides. Jenny hated to see him so frustrated. "Yes, I'm sure!" he returned. Neither Mister nor Jenny broached the reason why Todd felt so certain. But the suspicion of his sexual activity with Peggy added a new dimension to Jenny's attitude toward the proposed marriage. She felt motherly and protective toward both young people, and reluctantly she found part of herself silently consenting to the move.

"I was just over at her sister's house. That's where we usually meet," Todd explained. "And I told her the truth about my age. She's twenty-one. She doesn't care that I lied." He looked imploringly at his mother. "She loves me, Mom. And I love her so much my heart is breaking."

"I don't like the secrecy of it all," Mister asserted.

"We had no choice until we were sure she would be free. Don't you see, Pop?"

Mister's face showed weariness. He looked so frail, so tired, to Jenny. When their eyes met he said, "We can talk about this tomorrow, okay?"

Todd beseeched his mother. "Mom?" he said.

Jenny didn't know what to do. How could something like this be decided overnight? What could she and Mister say to each other that would make it easier? What could they say to him? She knew she should discourage her son, seeing in the way the lovelorn don't that he was in for hard times and maybe even more heartache. But what proof could she offer her strong-willed, intelligent son?

Dare she and Mister confront Todd with their own problem and thereby poison the very fiber of their family's stability? Did they simply wish him well and hope that by the time he reached their age, he'd at least have the love and trust his parents shared—even in the face of their personal dilemma?

Jenny sighed wearily and collapsed onto the vanity seat. She waved a limp hand toward her son. "We'll do as your father says, Todd. Tomorrow we might see things more clearly."

She was unprepared for the look of absolute accusation Todd gave her. It tore at her heart's moorings. He stormed quickly to the door. "I don't care!" he asserted, his still-lyrical voice cracking. "You're both hypocrites. And I'm not giving her up for anybody. I'm marrying her!" he screamed before slamming the door.

Mister caught Jenny in his arms before she had a chance to follow Todd. Immediately she saw the wisdom of waiting. What more could she add to their talk? She cried into Mister's shoulder. "I can't believe it. I can't believe what we've had to endure today!"

After they dressed, Mister and Jenny went down to check on the children. Joyce was helping Karen with a prop for a stage production she was involved with in school. Matthew was sitting, knees under his chin, absorbed in a space fantasy on TV. Amy was writing one of her secret letters to a school friend. And the baby was cooing at himself in the hall mirror. Todd was gone.

"What happened up there?" Joyce asked, alarming her mother until Jenny realized she was referring not to the sexual goings-on during "napping," but to the commotion with Todd.

Mister smiled a wan but tender smile. "Never mind," he admonished, seemingly unaffected by Joyce's huff. "That's between your brother and us—the same way your secrets are respected, too."

Jenny went into the kitchen, expecting to find a mess. Everything, down to the large pizza pan, was clean and tidy.

"They did all right without us," she told Mister over a cup of coffee later. A sadness rose in her chest. "I'm surprised." Then she broke into tears for what felt like the hundredth time that day. "Everything's changing, Mister," she whispered. "Everything in our lives is slipping into something else."

5

JENNY FELT MISTER'S bittersweet kiss on her cheek before he left for work. She lay, immobile and weary, watching the thoughts flit through her mind.

She remembered that Mister had told her he'd have to be at the gallery early to meet a seller, but for all the pinto beans in her pantry she could not remember what was being sold. Had he said it was an Afghan? Now what would that be, she wondered. A knitted lap-warmer? An emigré from Afghanistan seeking political asylum in Mister's shop? A wiry, frisky dog with unruly, shaggy hair? She wrapped the pillow around her head and moaned. Not a dog, she hoped. She had enough to do around the house without wrestling twelve-inch hairs from the vacuum cleaner.

She'd slept badly last night, listening to Mister's precious breathing and waiting for Todd's return, which wasn't until two A.M. She'd gotten out of bed to talk to her son, but at his bedroom door she'd developed a dread case of cold feet. She'd stood transfixed as she'd wondered what to say to him.

A day before—no, a half-day before—she would have been able to offer words of advice and empathy. She would have asked him to wait; she would have said that true love endures. But last night, with her feet growing literally and figuratively colder by the second, she'd felt a stranger to her own feelings. There seemed to be nothing she could say that would not automatically tune her emotions toward what she was experiencing with Mister, that would not expose her painful and vulnerable situation to her son.

No, what Todd needed was a clear-headed talk, not a weepy, emotional display that might only weaken his admiration and trust for his parents.

Back in bed, she'd gently touched Mister's shoulder, and she'd known that for all of her adult life her husband had been the measure against which she'd gauged all her heart's reckonings. Now she felt unanchored—without a frame of reference. She knew that their situation was serious because she didn't know *what* to feel. But before she'd drifted into a restless sleep, a wave of compassion for her husband had washed over her. He'd been harboring the very doubts she'd been free to voice. She must have seemed so selfish, so silly.

But this morning she felt no compassion. She was tired and angry and tense. How dare he resent their life? At least he got to dance! She'd spent the past nineteen years in service to others. She'd cleaned and organized and played nurse, acrobat, chef, chauffeur, counselor, lover, mother, and Grand Goose! For whom had she done it? For whom? her wild thoughts demanded.

There was a scuffling at her door. "I'll go in," she heard Joyce volunteer. "No, me!" Amy asserted. Then there were some hushed words of protest. Finally Karen called out, "Mommy?" Her gentle voice was so sweet. Jenny had named this one right, too. *Pure.* "Mommy, are you there?"

Jenny had to chuckle at the way fate always made a bigger fool of her than she could. Her question had been answered: she did what she did for her dear, miraculous children. Her children, who had been conceived in good

The Family Plan

faith. Her chuckle blossomed into an ironic laugh. "No!" she called. Oh, those innocent, lovely creatures!

"Then who's in Mommy's bed?" Matthew called through the old keyhole of the heavy wooden door. He could probably see lumpy covers and nothing else.

"The Ghost of Mothers Past!" Jenny called back spookily. If only those poor kids knew how close to the truth it was.

There was a stunned silence until Amy quipped, probably to a wide-eyed Matthew, "You're too young to understand Charles Dickens, Tiny Tim."

Jenny laughed into her quilt. Amy was so cute! And it was gratifying to know that she'd retained *some* of the story that Mister had read to the family, in chapters, two Christmases ago.

"Are you all right, Mommy?" Joyce whispered urgently.

Baby Lloyd awoke in his antique cradle at the foot of Jenny's bed. With a loud wail he let his conscious state be known.

"I knew it!" Matthew cried worriedly. "She got another baby! I told her not to kiss Daddy yesterday!"

The older girls laughed, but Amy hissed, "Oh, plug your blabber! Kissing does *not* give you babies!"

"Does too!"

"Does not!"

"Does too! And my mouth's getting tired of telling you so!"

"Mommy says it doesn't. And I believe her!"

"Yeah, well see?" Matthew reasoned. "She's got another one!"

Jenny scooped up baby Lloyd and appeared at the door. The four kids in the hall suddenly turned and went about their business once their mother's presence was assured. Such creatures of habit, Jenny marveled, identifying with them. In that instant she grasped the gravity of her situation and understood what it would mean to the kids if the family stability were threatened. Her own disorientation and anxiety were hint enough of what their reactions would be!

"See?" Amy made a point of telling Matthew as they raced to the bathroom. "It was only baby Lloyd!"

Matthew did an about-face and ran into Jenny's room. Only after a thorough search of the cradle, bed, and open dresser drawer did he look satisfied. Jenny shrugged as he passed her in the doorway. "And I was already getting to like the kid!" he complained.

She made the children a cold breakfast of unsweetened granola in fresh-pressed apple juice. After the kids left, she tidied the kitchen, nursed baby Lloyd, and stared blankly at the bright yellow walls. She felt no compulsion to straighten the sagging curtains someone had leaned against during breakfast. The romance was over between her and the smudges on the refrigerator. If she had felt discontent and malaise about her life before Mister's confession, what she felt now was a pain so fierce it was numbing.

The phone rang. Jenny hitched the baby under her arm and ran to answer it in the cozy darkness of the den. She didn't feel like talking in the kitchen; its brightness mocked her.

"Good morning, Jenny." That voice—it was Heddy Lock! Jenny was happy to hear from her, but she immediately admonished herself. After all, this was the object of her husband's torrid, if unrequited, desires. "Am I interrupting something?"

"Just a second," Jenny answered. "The milkman's here." Then, just an inch from the mouthpiece, she reprimanded, "Harvey, not my ears!"

Heddy was howling with delight. "Oh, Jenny," she enthused, "I wish I could bottle your humor. There's a world market for it, you know."

"They'd sue you for passing off hot air," Jenny rejoined, two distinct emotions welling up inside her. One of them was a warm and tugging desire to know Heddy better—as a woman, a friend, and Mister's colleague. They could have such fun together if it weren't for . . . the other emotion was an overpowering curiosity that bordered on the morbid—the feeling one got at the scene of an accident, or following a fire truck: Jenny wanted to follow the other woman, dissect her, discover where she had succeeded while Jenny had failed. In any event, both emotions drew her into the conversation.

"My husband, Paul, is coming out to Piper tonight," Heddy was saying, her voice betraying a certain tenseness, which, to Jenny's trained ear, sounded like forced nonchalance, "and I was wondering if you and Lloyd would care to join us for dinner. I mean, I figured one of your older kids could baby-sit..."

Jenny's nurturing nature couldn't stand the torture in the other woman's voice. "We can work it out," she assured her. "We never leave the care of the younger ones in our teenagers' hands—Lloyd's policy of giving everyone his freedom, you know—but, I'm sure I can find someone. And I'd love to meet your husband."

It was true. With the situation being what it was, meeting the man who'd married Heddy would be interesting enough. But now, with this added hint of things not being absolutely right in Lock Paradise, Jenny's natural curiosity was overwhelming her.

"Well, if you're sure. How does the West Room at the Lady K sound?" Heddy asked, her voice relieved and thankful.

"What's this?" Jenny heard Mister's voice approaching the phone. "Are you two woman subverting my authority?" he asked good-naturedly. Jenny's heart swelled as she envisioned her husband's laughing gray eyes and smiling lips. Wincing, she realized that any woman spending enough time with Lloyd Heath was bound to fall in love with him.

Oh, she wished she weren't at home in her bathrobe with her finger in the baby's mouth while Heddy—lucky Heddy Lock—shared the cramped, dusty gallery with Mister. She could just see his charming gestures, his sexy, sidelong glance, his strong shoulders straining his shirt fabric. Did he take off his sports jacket in Heddy's presence?

"Yes?" he asked into the phone, as though too distracted to acknowledge Jenny's existence enough to remember her name.

"Having fun?" she heard her bitter voice imply.

"Yes, darling. Heddy and I are just arguing about who makes decisions in a marriage: the wife or the husband."

"Arguing is for married people, don't forget," Jenny taunted. "First comes love, then comes marriage, then comes arguing over the baby carriage," she quoted Bea Kirke. "Didn't you ever hear that pithy aphorism, dear?"

Mister must have been sobered by Jenny's sarcasm, for his next words were delivered much less flippantly. She could just imagine his eyes narrowing as he caught on to his wife's mood. "Not in that version, I'm happy to say."

"Well, if I'd heard it early enough," Jenny began, her eyes burning with furious tears, "I might have saved myself almost nineteen years of devoting myself to a marriage that—" She stopped herself, gulped down her bitter-tasting words, and suppressed the tears.

"What's that?" Mister was saying, obviously for Heddy's benefit. "You don't think you can get a sitter tonight?"

"Mister," Jenny retorted, knowing full well that he was trying to spare her—and himself—the possible fiasco a dinner with the Locks might become, "I'll get a sitter if I have to hire a chimp from the zoo! I *want* to go out with them tonight." Her voice was cracking as she told him the truth. "How else am I supposed to keep on top of things, Lloyd? Please don't expect me to sit at home all day and concoct shameless suspicions."

Mister hummed for a second, and Jenny knew it was unfair to be putting him on the spot like this. But she knew no alternative. She didn't care if he couldn't present his side of the argument because of Heddy's presence.

"I'm sorry, Mister," she managed in a tight voice, "but I don't usually have occasion to defy you. Don't ruin my fun now."

"Well, that's fine, dear. Go check the toast before it burns. I'll explain to Heddy."

"Wait!" Jenny heard Heddy's panicky voice call. "Let me say good-bye." The next voice in Jenny's ear was Heddy's. "Oh, I did so hope you'd come," she cried, sounding frazzled and almost desperate.

The Family Plan

"We are, Heddy," Jenny assured her. "You must have misunderstood Lloyd. We were saying that we doubted we could find a baby-sitter for our three-week vacation this summer."

"Oh," Heddy responded. There was a short silence, during which Jenny could tell that she'd done a poor job of fooling the other woman. She wondered if Heddy suspected the same about her own attempt to appear nonchalant to Jenny. That would be an interesting turn of events, Jenny thought: two women tuning into each other's deepest fears. Heddy must have decided not to peer a gift horse in the mouth, because she sighed with what sounded like relief and said, "Great. See you tonight."

When Mister arrived home from work, the house was in an uproar. Jenny was whisking through it, trying to control the mayhem. She was dressed in straight-legged black knit slacks, a floppy cowl-neck robin's-egg-blue sweater with wide sleeves that flowed under her arms and along her sides to her waist, a black hand-tooled soft leather tunic that was belted at the waist with the same leather, and one simple black two-inch-heeled shoe. Limping, she directed traffic as Joyce and Karen maneuvered a huge painted backdrop through the kitchen.

Jenny smiled ruefully at Mister, knowing that she was in for trouble with him. "Turn your back on these kids for a minute and they create a monster like this," she hedged, hoping to get Mister to laugh, to chuckle, to even crack a line in his stony face.

Bea Kirke was washing a howling baby Lloyd in the kitchen sink. Mister nodded at Bea and offered to help. "No thanks, Mister Lloyd." Jenny loved to hear Bea call him that; it was the perfect meshing of both his names. "Compared to the hollering I've heard in my day, this baby's singing 'Yankee Doodle'!"

Jenny, watching eagerly, thought she saw a smile surface under Mister's facade. It was slight—just a light playing across his eyes and cheeks.

A loud crash seemed to stop all motion in the house—all except the baby's fussing. But then, babies had always been exempt from cares in the Heath household.

"It's Matthew and Amy," Jenny advised the others as she reached high to carefully bend a corner of the heavy cardboard scenery. A shower of electric-blue tempera paint settled in her hair. Standing on tiptoe in the shoed foot, she muttered patiently, "Why didn't you girls make this out in the garage?"

Karen's face was turning a bright red as she suppressed the urge to laugh at the sight of Jenny, all dressed to go out, sporting a layer of powdery paint. "Sorry, Mom," she whispered, her head bent. Then she let out one of her rare laughs of sweet, pealing delight. She tried to be apologetic as she murmured, "It looks very chic, Mom—goes well with your sweater."

"Yeah, well, maybe I'll start a trend in town among the other fashion-minded mothers."

"What the hell is going on upstairs?" Mister interjected.

"Nothing, darling," Jenny informed him as the girls' final tug freed the painting. They took it outside and laid it on the driveway for repairs. Jenny wiped her hands together and approached Mister. He regarded her with stern, authoritative eyes. As she sidled up to him, she whispered, "Is that murder I see in your gaze, dear?"

"For now it is. Until I think of something worse to do to you."

The next crash made even the baby stop fussing. Jenny grasped Mister's forearm. It felt so hard, so strong in her dainty hand. "Let them fight it out."

"Who?" Mister asked. "King Kong and Mighty Joe Young?"

Jenny couldn't believe that he wasn't even smiling. She laughed, throwing her head back. When she focused on her husband, she was knocked hard by the look of disgruntled desire in his eyes. Their smoky gray mist shrouded her in an almost tangible veil of grudging passion.

Jenny took advantage of the moment. She pressed herself

to him and peered up into his face. "C'mon," she coaxed, "you're smiling under there, aren't you?"

Mister turned to look up the stairs. Jenny hobbled around him and hopped up onto the first step so that she was eyeball-to-eyeball with him. Her face broadened into a mischievous grin. "There!" she approved of Mister's irrepressible smirk.

He lifted her up and placed her on the floor beside him. Then, two steps at a time, he began taking the stairs. "Don't try to charm me, Guinevere. Your name might mean fair lady in your name books, but in my book you're a sorceress."

Jenny immediately took up pursuit. She caught him at the bathroom door, where he was rattling the knob furiously. "Amy! Matthew! Open this door right now!"

Silence. Then slowly the door eased open, and Jenny saw a mess of towels, water, soap, and toiletries. Matthew dried his soaking head, looking triumphant. Amy was sputtering in frustration, her stitched lip quivering.

"He always wants to use the bathroom just when I want to!" she complained.

"And I always let you!" Matthew's pouty voice intoned. Then he pushed past his parents in a dignified trot. "But no more," he announced.

Jenny and Mister squatted down on their knees. Mister grabbed Matthew as he passed, and Jenny pressed a wet washcloth to Amy's face. Both parents were wiping away their children's tears of anger and frustration.

"You're not going to win all the time anymore!" Matthew accused his sister as his hands wrapped themselves in Mister's collar.

"I don't care!" Amy sputtered back, her tears wetting Jenny's sleeve.

"She's not so smart," Matthew cried to his father. "I'm smart, too."

"Yes, Matthew," Mister said, embracing him and then drawing both Amy and Jenny into his capable arms. "We're all smart..."—he glanced at his wife—"and dumb, in our own ways."

The children were left to clean up the mess as Jenny and Mister went into their bedroom. Mister threw his sports jacket over Jenny's vanity seat and crossed his arms. She loved him like this—a little tired, a little vulnerable, a little sexy, and very, very honest. "Looks like we're all demystifying something we thought was bigger than us. Even Matthew is finding out that Amy's only human."

Jenny bit her lower lip and nodded. She loved him so much! She loved his sweetness, his strength, his guts, his very being. "Looks like it," she agreed, smitten to the core by the poignant love she felt. "Everybody's changing."

She didn't expect Mister's next move. With two strides he was before her, lifting her off her feet, burying his head in her chest, kissing her face, her neck, her breasts through her leather and wool. He placed her on the bed and put a hand on each side of her. She was staring up at him like an innocent animal seeing a man for the first time.

Mister let out a huge sigh and fell softly onto his wife's body, crushing her beneath him and making the mattress dip. "Sometimes..." he began, his voice throaty and deep. He took a lock of her hair and twirled it between his thumb and forefinger, regarding it as though it were a precious swatch of ancient fabric, a delectable silk from ages past. "Sometimes when I look at you, I see just how much you've meant to me, and a strong urge to devour you, to hold you forever inside me, comes through."

"And sometimes," Jenny ventured, "I look like your old wife—the representation of all your ills, the cause of your imprisonment."

Mister leaned his face down to touch his soft, full lips to hers. They kissed for a seething moment, during which Jenny's hands clasped Mister's neck and head, forcing him closer. She knew the sensation he'd described; she knew it so well—she often wanted to eat him whole.

"And I?" Mister queried, "Am I your jailor?"

"You have looked like that to me on occasion," Jenny admitted. "Though I hate to think you see *me* the same way."

"Bad, isn't it," Mister commented, "when married people hold mirrors to each other. It makes for disillusionment."

Jenny smirked. "It can go either way, don't you think?" she asked. "If we create an illusion, we can make it disappear. All we have to change is our way of seeing our life."

Mister made a grand gesture with his hand. "That's all," he agreed, laughing. "What do you suggest we start with?"

She considered a moment, her mind flitting with her rapid thoughts. "I want a job," she said slowly. "I want a chance to prove that I can function outside of this relationship."

"Does the baby have his working papers yet?" Mister asked, reminding her of a difficulty she already knew too well.

"He'll be weaned soon," she offered.

"That'll help," Mister agreed.

"And you? What do you want?"

"You mean that's it? A simple job would make you happy?"

"It'd be a start. I've learned to be patient during my years of motherhood. Other things will follow."

"What I want," Mister confided, warming to the idea, "is to be free from having to do anything—at least for a while."

"We're making it sound so easy!" Jenny remarked. She looked directly into Mister's eyes and saw that he was aware that they'd been asking for things that were not as accessible as they sounded. Each of them stood at the peak of a huge pyramid composed of the intricate rocks and carvings that had brought their lives to their present states. If they jumped off . . .

Mister snuggled closer to her and brought his lips to her ear in a show of confidentiality. "What I really want," he whispered, "is to stop thinking about all of this—to just be Lloyd and Guinevere again."

Jenny didn't say anything. She just held on to his head and kissed him deeply. Yes, she wanted that, too; she wanted to go back to things the way they were. She didn't care if it meant ignoring something that was seething beneath the surface. What good did it do them to eat their problem for breakfast, lunch, and dinner? What did it give them besides a bitter taste and bad digestion?

They looked into each other's eyes. "All right," she agreed. "But I hope to heaven that we can work it out, Mister. Oh God, I hope we work it out!"

"C'mon," Mister urged, getting up and pulling her with him. "I'll call the Lady K and ask the maître d' to tell the Locks we'll be late."

Jenny chuckled. "Then you don't really mind going?"

Mister looked at his disheveled wife. She knew how she must look—blue flakes in her hair, her sleeves wet, her eye makeup streaked, her clothing crumpled—and it made her laugh. "I most certainly do mind," he said, already getting out of his work clothes and ready for a shower. "I also minded when Heddy asked me where we were going for summer vacation and I said we hadn't even thought of it yet."

Jenny began taking off her clothes for the shower, too. Her third that day! "Oh, I can imagine the scene that little white lie of mine must have caused," she exclaimed.

"In the future," Mister said, his eyes turned halfway toward his undressing wife, "please include me in any little deception you concoct."

Jenny slipped the black knit slacks off. "Well, you never expected the course of a proposed love affair to run smoothly, did you, Lloyd?" she asked, her eyes twinkling. "You were trying, over both Heddy's and my insistence, to change the tide of what we wanted. Oh, what a tangled web we weave when first we practice to deceive... our wives and mistresses," she added.

Mister tousled her hair, letting the sparkly blue flakes fall in a shower around her. "You need a refresher course in axioms, it seems," he teased.

"I get them from Bea, a woman with an advanced degree from the school of hard knocks," she taunted, finally kicking

The Family Plan

off her one shoe. As she followed Mister into the shower she muttered, "Where *is* the mate to that thing? I know the baby was chewing on the toe last week..."

6

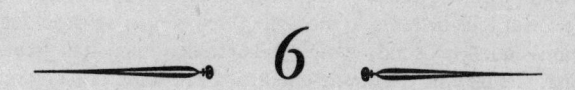

WHEN JENNY AND Mister finally made it to the hotel, Heddy was in the lobby, pacing in front of the main desk, her hands clasped behind her. As soon as she spotted them she glided over and embraced them both. Jenny's heart pounded painfully as she noticed that Mister closed his eyes in what was clearly a brief wish to savor the moment. Her head spun with fear and panic. Maybe she'd made a mistake—maybe it would have been better not to accept Heddy's invitation. Maybe it was true that ignorance was bliss, for she wished with all her might that she hadn't caught Mister's yearning expression.

Heddy linked her arm through each of theirs and led them toward the dining room. "Paul's already looking over the menu," she said. Jenny noticed that Heddy's voice was trembly, and she suspected it was with relief over having reinforcements on either side of her. "He only arrived in Piper an hour ago." She talked incessantly. "And I went for some fresh air while he used the shower in my room upstairs and changed, and, oh, there he is now, that's Paul."

Jenny cast a glance in Mister's direction. Evidently he was also noticing Heddy's nervousness. Mister gave Jenny a small shrug of his eyebrows that made his face look endearingly sexy. Then his eyes did a quick, secret scan of Paul Lock.

He saw them approach and stood up. His lean, muscular body easily reached six-foot-four, and he seemed unaccustomed to wearing a suit. If Jenny had considered Heddy dark, Paul made her appear fair and fragile. His curly black hair was parted on one side in a thick, unruly sweep. His eyebrows and moustache seemed to have been carefully placed on his face, hair by hair, in expressive arches by the hand of a benevolent creator who reveled in perfection.

Paul left the table to meet the three people approaching him, and as his solid, warm hand enfolded Jenny's in greeting, she had the disarming and heady sensation of being on his side, of cheering for him, of being immensely charmed.

Heddy disengaged her arms and, red-faced, made introductions. Mister, Jenny could see, was as surprised by Paul Lock as she. They shook hands in a strong, manly grip and gave each other polite, friendly grins that Jenny hoped would set the tone for the evening. As the party separated to be seated, Jenny saw that Mister, though strong and tall in his own right, looked like a kid brother beside Heddy's husband.

"My wife's been telling me some impressive things about you two," he told Jenny as he pulled a chair out for her.

Mister was helping Heddy get seated, and Jenny caught his slight attention to the fragrance of her hair. She smiled kindly at Paul, then changed her expression to a comical grimace of warning at Mister. "She claims you're the perfect couple," Paul was saying as he grated his chair closer to the table. "She has a certain fascination for the two of you."

"Paul!" Heddy scolded. "Leave them alone—you'll embarrass them."

Jenny smiled and winked at Heddy. "No, I'm very interested," she assured her.

Mister passed a wary hand over his face and then let it

The Family Plan 85

fall to the table, where it immediately took up drumming. He was probably thinking about the irony of it all: about how the Locks appeared to be in trouble while they admired a relationship that most certainly *was* in peril. "We've come to admire Heddy, too," he said, surprising Jenny with his frankness. Well, this evening was going to be very interesting indeed.

A small band was warming up. The cocktail waitress took their orders while the four of them made small talk about Mister's business and Heddy's role in it. There was a tangible tension between the Locks, and Jenny found herself feeling thankful for what was undoubtedly a rare camaraderie between herself and Mister—an understanding, a real friendship, that bound them together, even now, in the midst of trouble.

Heddy and Paul seemed to have the kind of relationship that hadn't yet had enough of what Jenny called binders—the cornstarch of marriage—its crises with children, a house, life, and death. They seemed to be a couple who were still dating, still feeling each other out, still unsure of each other's intentions and motives. The way Jenny and Mister might soon be feeling themselves, Jenny thought with dismay. It seemed all of life ran in a turbulent circle.

Jenny's nurturing side always came to the fore when she was around people in trouble. Tonight it was manifesting itself in glib jokes and good-natured self-deprecation. When Paul complimented her on her looks, she ruefully tugged at her curls. "I took three showers today," she told them, explaining, "Being a mother is dirty business! And my hair is rebelling. The more I wash it, the curlier it gets."

"But it's so becoming," Heddy said. "And I wish I had some curl in mine. It just hangs like a blanket. It's so bad."

"Well, if curly hair is good hair, when mine dies it'll go to Poodle Heaven," Jenny told her. The others laughed merrily.

"What did I tell you?" Heddy said to Paul. "Isn't she a marvel?"

Paul nodded through his chuckling and gave Jenny a

smile of appreciation. "My wife says you've raised six children," he began.

But before Jenny could answer, Heddy spouted, "Will you please stop calling me that."

Both Mister and Jenny stared in astonishment at Heddy. Paul took a patient breath and sighed. "All right," he said, his fists lightly landing on the tablecloth. "What should I call you? Am I allowed to say Mrs. Lock?"

Heddy was obviously embarrassed. She immediately began apologizing to Jenny and Mister, her clear amber eyes communicating a lost feeling. "I'm...I'm just sensitive about being called anything but my name," she explained.

Now Jenny was getting a clearer picture. Heddy was in a quandary similar to the one she herself was in. She intuitively guessed that Heddy was uncomfortable in her husband's presence because she probably felt the conflict most then. Alone, she was Heddy Lock, professional art dealer, capable businesswoman, independent traveler. In Paul's presence, she became his "wife."

Jenny rushed to Heddy's rescue. "It's such a generic term, isn't it?" she quipped. "Like canned peas with a white and black label." She shrugged to lesson the obviousness of her peace-making gesture.

But the gesture obviously hadn't escaped Heddy's notice. Her eyes turned toward Jenny in a slow, enlightened gaze, and Jenny knew that from that moment onward, their friendship was sealed in womanly blood.

Paul seemed to notice that something had transpired between the two women, because he gave each of them a crooked smile of unspoken acknowledgment. He stood up and asked Jenny to dance. Mister immediately followed suit.

Jenny's legs jerked in an involuntary attempt to forestall the intimacy the dancing would bring, but Heddy was already rising and slipping smoothly into Mister's arms. Jenny saw Mister's hand get lost behind the black curtain of the other woman's hair, and she wished she could monitor its movements.

She politely took Paul Lock's hand and let him whisk

her around the dance floor as she watched the other couple. Every once in a while they'd talk or laugh. Once Heddy looked sincerely into Mister's eyes, confiding in him. Jenny's blood was pounding in her head.

"Is that jealousy intuitive, or do you have reason?" Paul suddenly asked.

Jenny snapped out of her suspicious trance and regarded Paul. "I..." she began, at a loss for words as Paul smiled down at her. "I'm not jealous." She thought quickly. "You see, Lloyd..." Oh, what could she hope to say that wouldn't sound false to Paul's ears? Was she going to offer some lame lie the way she had to Heddy over the phone when they'd talk about baby-sitters? She shook her head and wet her lips. "I'm too used to reasoning with people who are a lot shorter than I am," she confessed. "They're perceptive, but nothing beats an adult's knack for honing in on the truth."

Paul suddenly pulled her closer and leaned his chin on her head. He took what sounded like a pained breath and asked, "Are you worried?"

Jenny felt her face flush so quickly that a sensation of light-headedness washed over her. Without looking into Paul's face, she shook her head against his chest. Then she muttered, "Not really, but Lloyd's at a crossroad. I only wish I could sneak him a marked map."

Paul gave a sweet laugh and said, "All roads would lead home, eh?"

Jenny pulled her head back and looked up at the man. "Yes," she answered truthfully. Then, at the momentary faraway glint in his eyes, she asked, "And you—do you worry about Heddy?"

"All the time," he sighed, answering without even thinking, it seemed. "She's so beautiful and so intelligent and so alluring and so..." He shrugged his massive shoulders. "And, you noticed, she's very protective of her freedom and her autonomy. And she can't seem to reconcile those ideas with a happy family life. My wife's threatened by my love for her."

"How odd!" Jenny cried. Then she reconsidered. "Actually, it makes sense, Paul."

"I know it does. How can she give herself fully to our personal future if it means giving up the things that are so important to her now?"

Jenny listened attentively. She empathized with the other woman's dilemma.

"She likes to say that her first marriage didn't work," Paul continued, "because she was too young. But I know better. She put her ex-husband off for the same reasons. She's so afraid of losing herself to love that she wrecks it for herself."

"Will you let her?" she asked.

Paul let out a chuckle. "I'm nuts about her. I might tell her this is her last chance, but I couldn't leave her. I just have to find a way to overcome her fears. And I'm starting right here, in Piper. I'm planting myself under her pretty little nose, and I'm not budging."

Paul's plan appealed to the romantic in Jenny. She knew that a lover needed to be loved. And it occurred to her that she should take a very active part in swaying Mister's feelings about her.

The music ended, but the conversation was so loaded and so important that neither Jenny nor Paul moved from the dance floor. They stood together for a moment, their arms still entwined, and both glanced at their table. Mister gave Jenny such a shocked look that she had to laugh. If only he knew what she and Paul were discussing! Heddy gave an unsure smile and a tiny wave. Jenny signaled for the other couple to join them on the dance floor, but she could see Heddy refusing Mister.

"They're on to us," Paul mused, smiling at Jenny as the next dance began. "They sense we've gotten chummy."

"I have to admit that I'm a little surprised by your frankness," Jenny said. "But since you started this, I'm going to be chummy, too." Her gaze flicked over Paul's face, getting the approval she looked for. "What are your chances together?" She caught her next breath in a tiny whistle. "Whew, that sounded franker than I expected!"

Paul was taking it all good-naturedly. "You're wondering how unhappy she is? How enticing another man's attentions might seem to her?"

Jenny felt her cheeks burn as the very doubts she'd been harboring found voice in Paul's words. "It does take two," she reasoned.

"I don't think she's got a thing for your husband, but she does admire him." He pulled back to look at Jenny. "And you."

"Well, Lloyd's feelings for her run a bit deeper than that, I'm afraid," she whispered against his shirt. "You see, he and I made the opposite choices you and Heddy made. We committed ourselves totally—and at a very young age. Now we're both wondering what we've missed—as you and she wonder what you *will* be missing."

She glanced over to their table, where she could sense that Mister was only half listening to what Heddy was saying, and a certain satisfaction filled her heart. Giggling, she muttered, "I think he's jealous that we're talking like this. Let's go join them." She pulled away, but Paul drew her closer.

Laughing, he said, "Let's not—jealousy's good for the circulation."

Jenny shook her head. "Initially it might work to incite your lover's emotions, but in the end it's detrimental. It gnaws at a relationship until it corrodes it entirely."

"You've had your share of it, I presume?" Paul asked as he spun her smoothly to the music.

Jenny shook her head. "Only lately."

"And Lloyd?"

Jenny tittered. "I'm not the cause of that kind of intrigue in our marriage. And he never was before this, either."

"Well, you have your theories and I have mine," Paul said as Jenny caught a glimpse of Mister standing and saying something to Heddy. "There's a law in relationships that says that the one who feels safest—the one who has the least to lose—is the one who controls it." Jenny looked from Mister to Paul. "I'm trying to swing the odds in my favor," he finished.

The dance ended, and Mister was advancing toward them. Jenny was shaking her head. "I hope you find out how beautiful it is when the control is in balance," she told Paul, her throat tight with grief over the changes her marital crisis had wrought. She whispered the next words just before Mister reached them. "I'm trying to even up the odds again."

Paul threw his arms up and surrendered Jenny with a smile of reluctance. She gave him a quick once-over to be sure their confidences were safe, and then turned into Mister's arms, her breasts meeting the familiar and beloved feel of his manly chest. Relief washed over her as she hugged her husband tightly.

"Very cozy," Mister remarked, his gray eyes murderous. He put both his hands on Jenny's shoulders as he drew her closer, and his palms wended their way into her mass of blond curls. "Interesting man, I take it?" Mister baited. "I picked up on a problem between them."

With a force that surprised Jenny, she found herself basking for a moment in the delicious knowledge that Mister was jealous. It was flattering and even briefly reassuring, and Jenny could understand how other couples resorted to provoking the emotion as a tactic to keep each other close. But she knew that in the long run, the only thing that made a relationship permanent and solid was the strength of the relationship itself.

"What were you talking about?" Mister queried.

Jenny didn't want to confide everything to Mister—at least not at this point in his fascination for Heddy. Something warned her against making Heddy sound like the poor victim in a struggle for freedom. If there was any emotion as potent as jealousy, it was sympathy for the object of one's desire. "You sensed the rift between them," she explained. "He was just telling me about it."

"She's acting like she needs our protection, isn't she?" Mister observed.

"Uh-huh," Jenny agreed. "They've got a lot to work out."

Then she squeezed herself against his body. "I'm so glad we're us," she whispered into his shoulder, that dear old friend of hers.

"So am I," Mister agreed, his twinkling eyes smiling down at her as he rocked her. "That way our clothes still fit us."

Jenny looked up into the wrinkles on Mister's chin as he stared at her, his head drawn back. "More than our clothes fit," she remarked wisely. "We're allies, aren't we, Mister?" He nodded. "Too bad you haven't had the opportunities I've had for comparing notes with other women—and even, just now, with Paul Lock."

"Sizing us up, eh?" he teased. "How do the Heaths measure?"

Jenny squinted up at her husband. "You won't believe it, but even with this trauma we're going through, we look pretty good."

Jenny smiled as they swirled to the music. She wouldn't have to set too many ideas into motion in Mister's perceptive brain. Heddy and Paul would be their own example of how *not* to run a marriage, and through his attraction to Heddy, Mister might come to appreciate better what he and Jenny already had.

Jenny didn't want the other woman to look bad; she sincerely liked her and harbored no bad feelings toward her. But, she thought with a measure of satisfaction, it was a good thing Mister was attracted to the kind of woman who was, deep down, very different from Jenny. Where Jenny was committed, fearless, and even adventuresome with the people she loved, Heddy pulled back. That would be enough.

Jenny's smile grew into a laugh as she leaned back against Mister's strong arms and parted her lips in enjoyment of the dance.

She suddenly became aware of Mister's stirrings as he sought to gather her hips closer to his own. "Sometimes you make my head spin, Guinevere!" he remarked as she leaned to weld her torso to his. Their foreheads were touching, their eyes locked.

"I want to keep it that way forever, Mister," she whispered, rubbing herself oh-so-subtly against him as they danced. "I want to keep it that way forever."

When the dance ended, they walked back to the table, each one holding the other's hand in a possessive clasp. There were problems between them, it was true, but they weren't really complaints about each other. Short of experimenting with freedom, Jenny could think of nothing to offer Mister—except what they already had, on different terms. But where would she start?

Dinner was brought by two waiters who took care of every detail and then stood back from the table, ready and waiting to serve.

"What line of work are you in?" Mister asked Paul after they made a meaningless, social wine toast. He was watching the other man closely, and Jenny wondered if it was out of concern for her or for Heddy.

Paul cast his wife a sidelong glance before he said, "Right now I'm open to new prospects, but I used to pipe oil for companies all over the country." He gave Heddy another glance before he added, "That's what first attracted Heddy to me, wasn't it?"

Heddy tossed her head in a semicircle, sending the mass of shiny black hair over her shoulders so that it settled like a sigh on her back. "It seemed like a good job for the husband of a roving art consultant to have." She looked at Jenny, who gave her a small smile. "No career conflicts."

"Well, there can't be marital problems if you can't find each other long enough to have a good fight," Jenny postulated, imagining the brutal schedule of prolonged absences the Locks' marriage must be subject to.

The other couple thought this very funny. "She's very astute," Paul told Mister, catching his eye and holding it— assessing him, Jenny guessed.

Mister gave Jenny a sudden smile. "Astute and cute," he murmured pleasantly, catching, Jenny hoped, a stronger whiff of the ill wind that blew between the other couple. Maybe that would make Heddy, by inference, a little less

The Family Plan

mystical and perfect in Mister's eyes.

"I quit that job last week," Paul was saying. "I want to devote myself to more—how shall I put this—domestic work."

Paul, Jenny knew, was suggesting that he wanted a family life. And hadn't Heddy confided over lunch yesterday that that was the very thing that terrified her?

Jenny was usually one who settled differences, but tonight she felt she should offer Heddy the other side of what having a family could be like. Yesterday she'd been tired and disillusioned, and she had spoken from that frame of reference. Now she took a chance.

"You and I could switch places, Paul," she began, knowing that, for their own personal reasons, each of the others was weighing her every word. "How would you like one eighteen-year-old who insists he's getting married in June, one baby who can't walk or talk yet, one seven-year-old who has just tonight come of age—very difficult period, you know; he's cut his idol down to size. She's a ten-year-old going on forty-one. Then you've got two teenage girls who imagine that everything has a sexual innuendo and who hog up all your books on every subject from horticulture to psychology."

Paul's eyes danced with merriment. Evidently, Jenny was describing the very things he wanted. "Sounds like a dream!"

"Ugh!" Heddy moaned, quickly adding, "No offense, Jenny!"

Paul remarked, "It must take a solid front to keep all that in line."

So he was getting in his licks, too. Oh, this certainly *was* very interesting! It gave Jenny goose bumps to contemplate the awesome decision Paul had made out of love for his wife. Because of his tenacity, the Locks had the potential for marital success. And, too, Jenny reasoned, they'd had what she and Mister never did—years of childlessness in which to get to know each other. If she and Mister had managed to build such a strong front with the distractions of family life, imagine the powerful bond this couple could make if they tried!

She smiled warmly at them, noticing their reticence with each other. In Mister's demeanor there was a certain caution, as if he knew Jenny was brewing one of her peace plots but wasn't quite sure where it would lead.

She decided to really shake up the dinner party. In her mind there were now more solutions than problems to this marital merry-go-round. "Watching our son—the one who wants to marry," she began, "I'm reminded that people in love think of marriage as the ultimate goal—the pot of gold at the end of the romance, the reason for all the courting, the kissing, the high-pitched fervor.

"And what do we do once we reach the goal?" she asked meaningfully. "Do we make all the fantasies come true? Do we take the opportunity to live, as they say, happily ever after?" She was talking quickly and with inspiration. She gave a tiny jump in her seat and turned toward Mister.

He was smiling ruefully at her. Gently, he lifted a hand and tugged on one of her curls until it straightened to its long blond length. "You're an eager evangelist for dirty diapers and household duties," he said softly, his voice simultaneously ironic and kind. "You surprise me, Jenny."

"Look, I know I've been rethinking my role in life," Jenny countered, "but, really, I believe in what I'm telling you. I know there's got to be a way to have both—a family life and a life outside."

"You see how hard it is," Mister began, but Jenny was shaking her head, cutting him off. She knew he was trying to keep her clear-headed and directed—attributes he'd instilled into the entire family. He was always the one who protected their integrity, sobered them when they got overzealous, lifted them and landed them, like an angel of mercy, safely on middle ground.

"You think I'm feeling this way temporarily," she intuited, "but I'm being very realistic." He'd like that. "I'm at the point where I know I'm not going to throw it all away. I want to make the changes I need from here,"—she pointed to both their hearts—"from inside our marriage."

Heddy must have felt that something vital was at stake. "It's probably a good life," she agreed, "if a family is what you want."

Paul gave her a glance so sulfurous Jenny could almost smell it across the table. "When you marry the person you've waited for all your life, you expect some kind of building to go on together," he put in.

Oh, now they were all getting somewhere. It was turning into a heated debate. The dinner was being left untouched as the four of them battled it out.

"Now, you, Jenny," Mister began, "haven't you been feeling that you want to get out into the world for a change?"

"Are you ever putting it delicately!" she exclaimed. "Twice a day I stop myself from calling the travel agent and booking a one-way ticket to Papua, New Guinea. Unfortunately, I don't have the money to suspend you and the kids in liquid nitrogen for the century I'd require. So the question is, how do I compromise?"

Heddy chose that moment to chime in, and Jenny suspected she was as much trying to make Jenny's wishes come true as she was trying to make a point to Paul. If vehement Jenny could be swayed, how strong could her convictions about marriage and children be? "You know, Jenny, I was thinking yesterday that it would be very helpful for Lloyd if you came to work at the gallery. There's so much work piled up in that back room, and he doesn't have time to organize, and eventually I'll be moving on..."

Now Jenny was in trouble; the proposal sounded so enticing. The idea of pointing out the merits of family life began evaporating. "Do you really think so?" she asked, her heart racing.

"Of course," Heddy responded. "And I tell you, even if you came this month while I'm there, we'd have enough work to keep us both on hot coals all day. We still haven't contacted the hotels along our Chinese itinerary or the art dealers or the out-of-the-way connections or the ministry of culture. Why, even the crating hasn't begun!"

Jenny looked to Mister, whose mouth was wide open. "Catching flies?" she asked. As his mouth formed an incredulous grin, she urged, "C'mon, Mister, you always said my time would come."

"Yes, but I never imagined it would come on *my* time," he remarked. "You don't even know anything about the business. I'd have to teach you everything."

"I'll get her started," Heddy argued. She was probably glorying in the example she'd made of Jenny; she couldn't have found a more willing specimen. "After all, aside from the expertise in art, running the gallery is like running any other business—"

"Or a household," Jenny put in, giving Paul a small smile she imagined would appear apologetic. "Imagine: I could run the shop whenever you were out of town, Lloyd."

Mister's eyes betrayed a small thrill at this last suggestion, and Jenny knew he was feeling the same bubbling-up that she'd been experiencing during these last incendiary moments.

Hadn't his wish been for the freedom to do whatever he pleased? This was working out beautifully! Who else would be more devoted to the cause of his business than the wife who depended upon it? And why shouldn't Jenny learn to help Mister? She'd come to expect his help at home, hadn't she? It seemed such a perfect step toward curing at least a small part of both their ills. It might only be a superficial move right now, but eventually, with more experience, they'd learn other ways to expand the atmosphere of freedom between them. And this particular step would still serve to bind them.

"Do you think you could handle everything at once?" he began. Jenny's heart leapt at the tone of reserved amusement in his voice.

"I could at least try," she ventured. "I only worry about the younger kids, but... well, let's try it, Lloyd. We'll see where it brings us."

"Have you ever worked before?" Paul asked, nervously smoothing his moustache with two fingers.

Heddy's delicate palm hit the table. "What is this? An interview?"

Jenny smothered a giggle. "No," she answered Paul, "but as a mother of six and the wife of a father of six, I've picked up some skills."

"What about the children?" he pointed out. "They'll need someone around."

"Paul," Heddy warned, "you're acting like a mother hen. Jenny's children are old enough to take care of themselves when they get home from school."

"Can the baby get his own beer from the refrigerator?" Paul countered sardonically.

Jenny laughed at the image, and Mister mused aloud, "He could come to work with us."

"But what about the others?" Paul insisted, trying, Jenny guessed, to make a case for his own pet cause: the raising of a family. "They should have a say in—" He didn't get far; the other three at the table took up a heated exchange.

"That's just it!" Jenny emoted. "We all should."

"Absolutely, Paul," Heddy contended. "That's what I've been getting at. Jenny shouldn't have to have a certain life flung at her from Lloyd—"

Both Mister and Paul tried to interrupt; Paul won out. "But," he insisted, "the family's the basic unit—"

"Oh shut up!" Heddy shouted, her hair swaying violently from one side to the other as her head took opposite directions.

Everyone in the restaurant stopped talking to stare at the four maniacs arguing as their food iced over.

The waiters, who were so engrossed in the talk that they'd slowly inched their way closer to the group, now stared at each other in obvious shock.

Amid the sudden silence, Jenny, Mister, Heddy, and Paul began laughing. They laughed until tears were streaming down their faces, and they reached across the table to hold trembling hands, like in a seance that had just succeeded in exorcising mischievous poltergeists.

"I told you they were fun," Heddy whispered loudly to Paul.

7

WHEN JENNY AND Mister arrived home, the house was very quiet. They went into their bedroom and closed the door.

"Can I start tomorrow?" Jenny asked as she brushed her hair at the vanity. It sprang out in a soft bushy mass that tickled her neck and ears. In the mirror she could see baby Lloyd sleeping in his cradle at the foot of the ancient matrimonial bed.

Mister stooped to tuck the baby's cover under his pudgy chin. "I should think you'd be more sensitive to the situation," he said in a remote voice as he turned down the quilt and covers of their big bed.

"What situation?" Jenny asked, her hands freezing in their motion of passing the heavy brush through her mane.

Mister let out a huge sigh and disappeared into the bathroom.

Jenny sat transfixed at the mirror. "What situation?" she repeated.

"Heddy," came the single word reply.

Jenny breathed deeply, trying to calm herself and seriously consider an appropriate response. "Did you see the things I saw tonight? You know, how coolly Heddy acts toward Paul?"

Mister emerged from the bathroom, his toothbrush in hand, his teal-blue bath sheet around his neck like a huge yoke. "She's caught between two worlds," he began as he leaned againt the doorjamb. "The way I am. The way *you* are," he pointed out. "And Paul is trying to push something on her that she doesn't want."

Jenny swung herself around to face him. "Don't try to turn her into a victim, Lloyd," she said calmly and smoothly. "Their problems together are more complicated than you or I could probably guess. And they're not all Paul's fault. She's had something to do with creating their situation."

Mister regarded Jenny quietly for a split second. Then his face broke into an amused smirk. "You don't believe I'm capable of being unfaithful, do you?"

"I wouldn't want to test you on it," she returned. "But then, where would you find a woman as perfectly suited to you as I am?" she said lightly. Slightly more seriously, she added, "You know, I don't think Heddy's the threat. The real problem is that you're attracted to her at all. I mean, if one woman can catch your eye, what's to say another can't? And maybe that one might not turn out to be a friend—to you or me."

"She'd have to be pretty smashing," Mister remarked as he sauntered over to Jenny.

She leaned back, her elbows resting on the vanity. "That's a compliment, I take it." Mister's gray eyes assessed his wife, looking at her as though she were suddenly new to him. Jenny felt the heat rising from deep within her. It flushed her skin and ran its velvety fingers over her breasts. "But," she began, slightly tensed, "I want *you* to feel that no one could ever take my place. I get the feeling you're taking me for granted, Lloyd Heath." She planted her feet firmly and bolted up, out of his reach. "Let's see what it's like for you to spend a night without me," she called, racing out of the room and down the stairs.

The Family Plan

Mister's footfalls were close behind her as she reached the den door and slammed it before he could get in.

Laughing in the darkness, she yanked one of the TV blankets out of the chest and plopped down onto the couch. Immediately she was aware of someone beneath her. One of the kids must have fallen asleep in front of the TV. What would she do now if Mister tried to storm the door?

"Ow!" came a thick voice.

"Bea?" she whispered.

There was a rattling at the den door. Mister had retrieved the master key from the knife drawer in the kitchen.

"Well, if it's not me, I'm in trouble," Bea answered.

Jenny turned on the light, expecting to find that Bea had fallen asleep while baby-sitting. But not only was she dressed for bed, her hair was also set in bobby pins.

Mister opened the door triumphantly, but his expression was soon displaced by bewilderment. "Hello, Beatrice," he muttered politely, as though nothing at all strange were going on. "Thank you for staying so late. Jenny and I have things under control now."

"I'm not going home," Bea stated.

Jenny and Mister stared at each other. "No?" Jenny asked gingerly. "What are you doing?"

"I was doing a life sentence, but I've computed it."

"Commuted," Mister corrected automatically.

"No, I've computed it," she replied. "And the way I figure it, I lost time and money every year." She yawned and sank down into the covers, her ample right hip hanging off the edge of the couch.

"I'm sure you did," Jenny exclaimed, secretly relieved that her friend and housekeeper had finally freed herself from the shackles of a stinky marriage.

"Jenny!" Mister scolded. "Don't make matters worse."

Bea opened one eye and looked at Mister as though he were crazy. "She couldn't make them any worse than they already were, Mister Lloyd. Now if you folks would go have your fight elsewhere, I'll get some sleep. I have to work in the morning."

"What fight?" Mister asked.

Bea opened her eye again and gave Mister one of her Don't-try-to-put-one-over-on-me glares. Mister, somewhat wilted but still dignified, took a step backward.

"Well, how long can you stay?" Mister asked gingerly.

Bea looked at Jenny. "Doesn't he ever come out and say exactly what he means?" she asked.

"It's his name," Jenny confided.

"Oh," Bea answered knowingly. "A parent should be more careful what name a kid gets haunted with. Gray," she mused aloud. "Dark." Then she sat up and straightened the heavy mass of metal pins in her hair. "No use trying to sleep when there's fighting to be done," she philosophized. "I'll figure out a place to stay and be out of here by morning," she assured the Heaths. "I'd stay with my married son, but then I'd have to take two buses to Piper every morning to work for the folks here. I'd stay with my daughter, but then I'd just have to eat I-told-you-so for breakfast, lunch, and dinner. Some diet! I could—"

"Wait!" Jenny exclaimed. "You could stay with us—isn't that right, Mister? I'll be working at the gallery starting tomorrow." The idea was sounding better by the minute. "I'll take the baby with me. After all, there isn't much business from off the streets, and he sleeps most of the time. Oh, Bea, this is perfect!"

"I'd still have to take care of my other customers during the day," she asserted. "A woman can't put all her apples in one henhouse," she reminded them.

Mister hit his palm to his forehead, more over the mixed metaphor than the mixed-up situation, Jenny guessed.

"Then every night I could come home here and start supper," Bea said, clearly warming to the idea as much as Jenny was. "Then I'd baby-sit nights if you needed me to, or I'd get out of your hair..."

"We'll clean out the attic, Bea," Jenny encouraged. "It's as big as the whole upstairs, and insulated, too. You could use the kids' bathroom if you don't mind space toys in your bath and soggy towels on the floor. These old houses—

The Family Plan

they never had enough baths."

Mister beat a retreat, and Jenny and Bea discussed the merits of the plan for another few minutes before they hugged and bade each other good night.

Up in her bedroom, Jenny got into bed beside Mister and turned her back to him. Mister tossed for a while and then pressed up against her back. She could feel his stirrings. He was like a caged animal in heat, but to Jenny, making love right now was too dangerous. She would never know if Mister was thinking of her or of Heddy Lock. And even though she truly felt that Heddy was merely a representation of subtler ills, the problem of Mister's turmoil still remained.

Heddy Lock wasn't the enemy. Mister's uneasiness, his sense, as he had put it, of "What now?"—these were the things to be reckoned with. So for once Jenny didn't encourage Mister's urgings. She lay thinking and musing as he sought to excite her unwilling body.

Consciously, she felt she understood Mister's attraction to Heddy. She'd succeeded in doing something extremely difficult in the world of art dealers. She'd succeeded in doing what he hadn't. Even though they had similar interests, backgrounds, and training, Mister was largely tied to the gallery so that he could provide support for Jenny and stability for the children.

Heddy, on the other hand, was free to offer her services as a roving consultant to others in the art world. She could choose among many exciting jobs, unencumbered by inventory.

And though Mister did travel often, the travel headaches and expenses were all his. The things to be lost or gained were his, too. And, too, he was not free to roam in leisure after his business had been transacted. He often said he'd visited not the countries but the hotels and conference rooms of the world. It was hard enough feeling as Jenny did— that the planet lay out there ready for her exciting adventures to take place. She could only imagine Mister's frustrations of having it so close and yet untouchable. He always had to come home.

And as far as Mister's amorous feelings for the other woman went, in an oddly reassuring way Jenny felt safe. She suspected something very distinct from love was transpiring. The way he'd defended Heddy tonight, the way he'd wanted—but failed, luckily—to dislike Paul, the way he'd become, for the first time Jenny could remember, actually jealous over her interactions with another man—all these things indicated not that he was in love, but that he was defending changes within himself.

Jenny began having trouble fitting the pieces together. She would like to have said that she was too tired to think, but the truth was that Mister's probing, roving hands were making the downy hairs on her arms stand on end. They were making the normally stable processes of breathing and sleeping and analyzing impossible.

And his sweet cooings, his tender words, were making her believe in him again. She'd been worried before tonight, and she'd been confused. But now, now that she saw that all of life was one big change—that despite his frustrations, Mister still loved her, that Bea Kirke was leaving her husband, that an oil laborer wanted to be a househusband and father, that Heddy felt a special affection for Jenny—now she felt that the only thing that seemed true was whatever was happening at any given moment. And at this moment, Mister—that sexy, frustrating, masterful man—was whispering her name, asking her to give him time.

"Please, Jenny," he was whispering into her ear, and his warm breath enveloped it in sweet passion. "Just flow with me; let's see this thing through to its end. Just give me some time, darling, Just time."

Jenny turned over so that she was facing her husband. His head went beneath the sheets to gently nudge her breasts, and as he did so Jenny remembered that she hadn't nursed since this morning. And baby Lloyd had not complained, Bea had mentioned. She felt Mister's lips nibble at her ribs, and then his expert hands lifted her nightgown up over her hips. "What are you thinking, Mister?" she whispered as his head emerged to glue their lips together.

The Family Plan

Mister gave a drugged smile, his gray eyes looking deeply into hers. "I'm thinking of you, Jenny," he answered. "Oh God!" he exclaimed as his lips crushed hers and his tongue seethed in her mouth. He backed off long enough to say, "Believe me, Jenny. I've never wanted to think of anyone but you!"

It was a little strange and a little exciting for Jenny to be dressing instead of making breakfast the next morning. She couldn't suppress her merry feelings as Mister, shaking his head, watched her dress the baby.

"Mommy's all grown-up today," she teased the child, "and you and she are going to work for Daddy."

"Welcome to the human race, son," Mister said as he passed the bed on his way to the bathroom.

Jenny turned from wedging the jumpsuit onto the baby and fell into her husband's arms. Her hands reached around his neck as his clean-shaven, cologned, and firm face rubbed gruffly against her softness. Mister molded his lips to hers and wrapped his arms completely around her.

"We'll have fun together," Jenny promised. Then she cast her eyes upward to his. "Thanks for the chance," she murmured.

"I'm leaving you in Heddy's hands," Mister said. "You two can invent all the faults you want to right."

A shiver of anticipation ran up Jenny's spine. She hadn't really considered what it would be like working with the other woman. For a moment she felt a giddy excitement—as if she and Heddy were meeting for a grand spree on the town. She also felt a certain anxiety. What if she saw things she wished to be insulated from? What if she noticed, as she had last night, Mister's subtle attraction to Heddy?

She pulled away from Mister and tended to baby Lloyd. It was something she'd have to confront, this semi-infatuation of Mister's. Something she had to be there not only to observe, but to prevent from growing.

When they went downstairs, they were faced with an uproar in the kitchen. Apparently none of the children could figure out what Bea Kirke was doing waddling around in her bathrobe at such an hour. Jenny saw Joyce and Karen warily showing Bea just how thoroughly cooked the family liked its eggs. Amy was explaining that both the toaster and the toaster oven were needed to meet the Heaths' ravenous demand for whole wheat toast. Matthew was standing on a chair, his shirt front tightly tucked in and bulging with just-picked apples.

"You cut them up and push them through and then you have it," he said, looking up into Bea's face. "What are those little antennae in your hair for? Is there a receiver in your tooth fillings?"

Bea patted him on the head as she reached for the salt shaker. The many-voiced cry of "No salt!" rang through the kitchen. Replacing the thing, Bea regarded Matthew. "No," she informed him. "I sleep plugged into a machine that gives me ideas about how to handle tough little kids."

"Oh, I can't believe that," Matthew retorted. "I know what electrodes look like, and those are antennae, not electrodes." Satisfied, he hopped off the chair and almost crashed into Jenny's legs.

"Mrs. Kirke will be staying with us," Mister announced as he poured himself a cup of coffee and held the pot high, offering some to Jenny. "Please cooperate with her, as I see you already are." He seemed pleased with his children until Matthew piped, "I'm going to spy on her when she's sleeping."

"Don't you dare!" Jenny warned. Matthew simply looked more determined, and she knew it would be useless to try to persuade him that there was nothing amiss about Bea's sleeping habits. He loved any intrigue that had to do with technology or espionage, preferably both.

"They're bobby pins, dopey," Joyce informed her little brother as she counted out vitamin pills for herself and Karen.

"What are you girls taking?" Mister asked.

Joyce read the label: "'Mystery Tabs.' They're supposed to be excellent for the hair and teeth."

"What's in them?" her father persisted, taking the bottle from her. Scrutinizing the label, he frowned.

Amy had stopped eating to observe her father. "They're called Mystery Tabs because no one can figure out what's in them," she noted.

"What's bobby pins?" Matthew persisted, his nose wrinkling the way it did when any new bit of information sounded suspect.

Jenny explained their purpose and then added, "I saw Mrs. Kirke sleeping last night myself. There's absolutely nothing to her contention that she sleeps with a machine."

Joyce and Karen laughed, and Jenny could only guess why.

Bea took a cup of coffee and sat on the bench alongside the window. She gave Jenny a careful look that communicated motherly concern. Jenny returned the gaze with increasing curiosity, letting Bea know that she should come out with whatever it was she had to say.

"You didn't have to sit on me last night," Bea began. "There was a free bed in the house."

Jenny froze for a second and cast her gaze around the table. Apparently Karen had heard Bea, because she asked suddenly, "Where's Todd?"

Mister's chair scraped the yellow-tiled floor as his body shot up to take the stairs two at a time. Jenny scooped up baby Lloyd, who'd been frightened by the commotion, and went to stand at the foot of the steps. When Mister appeared at the top, his head was low, his eyes menacing, his expression stern.

His feet rumbled down the stairs. He grabbed Jenny by the arm, yanked her jacket and the baby's blanket off the coat hooks at the door, and coaxed them hurriedly toward his car.

Bea was at the door, her eyes concerned. The children stood around her, their mouths agape. "You can reach us at the shop, Bea," Mister called out as he revved the engine and headed down the driveway.

Jenny buckled herself and the baby into the seat belt.

Her heart was pounding with fear and dread. "Nothing?" she asked, referring to what Mister had found in Todd's room.

Mister didn't take his eyes off the road. He shook his head no and shot Jenny a glance that she knew was intended for their son. "What's this Peggy's last name?"

Jenny searched her mind, only to be dismayed by the lack of information she had on the girl. She knew only that Todd and she had been meeting at Peggy's older sister's, and that Peggy was in the process of getting an annulment. Oh, Todd! That young and precious child! If Jenny had her hands on him now, he'd be turning blue from lack of air.

Mister slowed down as he reached the high school crossing zone. There were some kids hanging around outside, but it was still too early for the morning crunch. He swung into a space marked RESERVED, ran around to open Jenny's door, and marched them all into the school office.

Jenny recognized a girl—a friend of Todd's—sitting at the attendance desk. The girl amost smiled, but then a cloud that said "The game is up" descended over her pretty face.

Mister introduced himself and Jenny to the attendance monitor, who gave them a reception they hadn't expected. "Well, it's about time!" she exclaimed. "If Todd weren't such a well-dressed, perfectly mannered boy, I'd believe he was an orphan!"

To their consternation and surprise, the woman explained that she'd been having their house called every day. "Since school started three weeks ago your son has appeared four times."

"Why, that's impossible!" Jenny began. Then the light started to dawn as she caught Todd's friend slinking out of her seat. She remembered her name. "Cynthia, are you responsible for making the calls?"

The girl looked sheepish while the monitor almost fell off her chair at the realization of what had been happening. "But, but," she sputtered, "you're an honor student."

"And so is—well—so was Todd," Mister said. "Evidently honor students aren't always honorable."

The Family Plan

They discussed the problem inside and out until the bell rang for the first class, taking a tearful Cynthia with it. She was going to be reported, and her parents would learn of what she'd done.

"But that doesn't excuse or help find our son," Jenny asserted. "It wouldn't be so hard to take if we didn't trust him—all our children—so completely."

Cynthia had not been able to provide any information about Todd's whereabouts during his absences from school. Jenny had believed her, though in doing so, another disappointment over Todd had surfaced. He'd probably been leading this girl on, never telling her his reasons, so that she'd do his bidding.

When Jenny and Mister visited the principal, the school official asked them where Todd might be but was no help in piecing together the identity or whereabouts of Peggy or her sister—about whom the Heaths knew even less. "It probably started as a summer thing," Jenny explained. "Todd may have met Peggy while he was working at the golf course at the Lady K." She looked down into her lap, where the baby lay staring out at the world of which he knew so very little. Jenny didn't volunteer the information that Peggy had been married. What difference would it have made to the principal, who could offer no help?

After the inconclusive meeting, Jenny and Mister drove around town, checked at the country club, asked at the Mexican restaurant, and even cruised the residential neighborhoods. Each parent was lost in thought over Todd, the fox. Neither Jenny nor Mister spoke as they scanned the streets for any sign of their handsome son, who until now—until he'd fallen so desperately in love—had always been the very model of competence, good breeding, and sensibility.

Everyone loved him, everyone trusted him—everyone from his doting, blind parents, Jenny thought, to shy Karen, to the girls at school. Girls like Cynthia, who apparently would have done anything for one of his devilishly engaging smiles.

When there seemed nowhere else to go, they drove to Mister's gallery in the elegant section of town, parked in the private driveway, and went inside.

Heddy was on the phone. "It's Bea Kirke," she told them. Evidently Bea had explained the situation to Heddy.

Jenny rushed to the phone, but Bea was calling only to check. She was at another job and wanted to be able to work with peace of mind.

Jenny phoned home, but the hollow ringing made her visualize her perfect house—empty. Each room carefully done in periods from ages gone by. Each bed still disheveled—except for Todd's. Each plant hanging still in the lonely windows that had not been opened. A melancholy feeling gripped her as she limply hung up the phone.

Heddy looked into Jenny's face. Mister had gone to put on a pot of coffee, and the two women were alone in the cluttered, sunny back office that oozed culture, refinement, and a certain comfortable stuffiness that were characteristic of Lloyd Heath. The sincere empathy in Heddy's gaze, the sunlight shining on her jet-black hair, the quiet insulation of all the sundry objects around her, made Jenny start weeping.

"I don't know what's happened to my family," she began. Bitter-tasting tears ran into her mouth, and the baby on her lap, as if sensing his mother's anxiety, punched his tiny fist at her face. She looked at Heddy, and the two of them gave pained little chuckles that made Jenny's tears flow more freely and the waiting ones in Heddy's eyes finally surface.

Jenny sniffled, trying to summon up a smile, and wiped her eyes on the corner of the baby's blanket. "I've been so wrapped up in my own crises that I didn't even notice this beam up my backside," she joked.

Heddy giggled as she wiped her own tears on a hanky she had tucked into her sleeve. "Being a mother has got to be the toughest job there is," she said. "I don't think I could handle it. It's just so scary, so awesome."

Jenny was dabbing her cheeks and taking a deep breath.

"Oh, but it's the most beautiful thing in the world, Heddy!" Then she laughed at herself; just a second ago she'd been lamenting her plight. "If you can overlook the heartbreak," she concluded wryly.

Mister came into the office just as the two of them were laughing at their fears. "What have I gotten myself into?" he groaned. "I hope you two don't start sending out invitations to these little hen parties back here; I don't think I could stand the cackling."

He pulled his handkerchief from his back pocket and dabbed first Jenny's face and then, very delicately, Jenny thought, Heddy's. She wondered if Heddy caught the scent of the kerchief that smelled so beguilingly of Mister.

"Get out of here, Mr. Heath," Heddy instructed as she backed him out of the tiny, overcrowded space. "Only human beings with hearts are allowed, and you're being heartless."

"Hey, I resent this," he complained.

Jenny knew her husband well enough to pick up the hurt in his joking voice. Everyone treated him like the faithful pet Schnauzer. It made her knowledge of her husband's wondrous spirit that much more special. "Let him stay," Jenny conceded, "He's one of us."

Mister adjusted his jacket—so he did keep it on in Heddy's presence!—and swiped at an imaginary piece of lint. Jenny had to laugh. "Oh sit down, Mister," she told him. "You're the biggest sap on your side of the genders."

By mid-morning Jenny had discovered that she liked the way Heddy and Mister related to each other. They were professionals, colleagues with a strong mutual understanding.

Heddy was out front organizing some pieces they intended to take to China to trade or sell there when Mister began flipping through his address file, tossing an occasional card into Jenny's lap. She put the baby into his carrier in the sunlight and sat down to see what kind of work Mister was giving her to do.

The names on the cards were all of friends of Todd's. She surmised that Mister had had them since the days when he'd coached his son's summer baseball team. Together they made all the calls but turned up nothing.

Temporarily resigned, Jenny straightened up, her back stiff and sore, and decided to start learning the ropes in the gallery. She sauntered out to find Heddy, who answered her interest with a detailed description of how the cataloguing system worked.

Jenny spent the rest of the day helping Heddy, occasionally making more dead-end calls about Todd, reorganizing Mister's completely mixed-up address cards, and fixing the mechanism in the drip coffee pot that had not worked properly, Mister informed her, since a week after she'd bought it for the gallery last year.

"You see?" Heddy remarked when the three of them had put down their work for a break. "In one day Jenny has cured some very bothersome ills."

Mister gave his wife one of his crooked smiles that never failed to melt her heart. She could see that he was relieved not to feel uncomfortable working around the two women who attracted him. He probably felt somewhat ambivalent over her blossoming friendship with Heddy and their uncanny understanding of each other.

She wondered if he had any intentions of doing something about the confusion he was experiencing. He was certainly not the type of man to behave recklessly when other people's futures were at stake.

Still, would he ever profess his feelings for Heddy? Was he perhaps waiting for a moment when—in China, and light years away from their respective lives—he could broach the subject? Or would he let go of the idea of Heddy—just let his desires fester and grow?

8

WHEN THEY ARRIVED home that night, Todd was in his room, lying on the bed and listening to his earphones, which were now hooked up to his stereo system. Even standing at his door, a distance of ten feet away, Jenny heard the hard, gutsy song she sometimes danced to while doing housework. It was a song of lamentation, a song that said that no one should be shackled, that the singer was made for life on the run, life on the edge, life where all old rules were invalid.

Jenny listened for a moment, thinking about the song lyrics with which she'd often identified, but Mister calmly went to the stereo, snapped it off, and stood towering over the reclining Todd.

It surprised Jenny to see how serenely Todd regarded his father. Evidently, in knowing that the moment of truth had arrived, Todd was going to be direct. He didn't smile, he didn't move, but his lower lip quivered slightly as he stared at his father, a poignant picture of his older, future self.

"Get up," Mister commanded softly.

Todd didn't obey.

Jenny sensed big trouble. She sidled over to Todd's bedside and pleaded with her eyes. Todd's handsome, smooth face that had not yet lost a certain soft quality was upturned toward his mother's anguished one. His Adam's apple bobbed once before he said, "I'm going to marry Peggy, Mom, whether you or Pop like it or not."

And Jenny knew it was true. She knew what Todd felt; she understood his fervor, his great enthusiasm for love. All she could do was close her eyes and give a little nod that embodied her memories: the sweetness of young love with Mister; the drama of their eventful lives; the joyous, blissful births of their children; the aching deep desire for her husband; and now, the terrifying fear that she was losing the interest of the only man she'd ever loved.

She wasn't necessarily losing him to another woman—that would be easy to fight with love and patience and a bleeding heart. No, she was losing Mister to a dream like Todd's; she was losing Mister to the dream of another dream. And she suspected that the hour of reckoning was near; that she'd have to—before the China trip—make Mister understand that their marriage could handle conflict, could survive it.

"You're not going anywhere and you're not doing anything. You're not even going to go to the john unescorted, young man," Mister warned, his voice bringing Jenny back to the present.

"Mister, please," Jenny pleaded. "Don't you remember? Don't you—"

"Mom," Todd said, his voice frighteningly calm. "Let him. I don't care. Because with or without his approval, I'm—"

"Jenny," Mister said, his eyes riveting his son, "let me talk to him alone."

"But it's dinnertime, Lloyd. Can't it wait? Bea has made your favorite—"

The look Mister shot her made her skin crawl. She nodded at her son, who looked vulnerable even as he gave her a firm nod, but still she didn't move.

The Family Plan 115

She resented being dismissed while Mister took care of a problem that was intrinsically hers, too. Her instinct for keeping the family stable—for accommodating Mister as he often accommodated her—made her waver for a moment, but she stood her ground.

"I'd like to stay," she murmured softly enough to cover her rebellious determination. Mister's eyes locked with hers. "I'm sure you understand," she asserted.

Todd's gaze darted from his mother to his father. Swiftly he sat up, pulling his earphones down so that they formed a metal collar around his neck. "There's nothing you can say to change my mind," he addressed to his father.

"Listen, Todd," Mister began sternly, "what do you know about life? What kind of preparation do you have for marriage and a family? You don't even know what kind of work you want to do. You don't have any idea of what's beyond these protected walls and the circle of this family."

"I know as much as I need to," Todd asserted.

Jenny's voice was slightly shaky as she put in, "And what's that?"

"I know I love Peggy. I know that I don't want to be without her. That even right now I'm dying inside because she's off in the city, getting some of her papers together and meeting with her husband."

Her son's words made themselves felt in Jenny's heart. Silently she accepted Todd's sentiments. She turned to show Mister her compassion for their boy when she noticed that for her husband, the issue was very fiery and nowhere near resolved.

Mister sat down on the bed beside Todd, but there was no softening in him, no resignation that Jenny could determine. "I know this is going to sound harsh," he began, his voice dangerously soft, "and I know I've never done this to you before, son, but I have to step in here. For your own good."

"Wait a minute," Todd protested, his voice trembling with defiance.

"No, you wait," Mister said calmly. He looked at Jenny,

signaling her to please leave. In his gray eyes Jenny saw frustration and pleading. However, instead of spurring her to leave, Mister's demeanor intrigued her to stay. She sensed they were on to something, that he wanted her to leave so he could confide something very special to their son—and there was no way she was going to miss this revelation. She shook her head.

Mister took a deep breath, began to say something, and then apparently thought better of it. "Okay," he addressed Todd. "Let's say you marry Peggy now. Let's say you have a nice life—that you get your share of ups and downs, that you have—well—a good life. I'll start from that point, all right?" Todd nodded expectantly. "I won't even bother talking about a bad life, or the ugliness that could result if you two end up not really knowing or understanding each other, or not growing together—God, you're both still so young!—or of having any kind of catastrophe happen." He swatted the air around his head. "Let's start from the place where you stand right now: a young man very much in love, very hopeful, very optimistic. Okay?"

He looked to both his son and his wife, and Jenny sensed that Mister was taking a risk with what he was about to say.

"My point is, Todd," he continued, "that you and Peggy will start to build a lot of things between you. Oh, I don't mean material things. I don't even want to cloud this issue with the idea of a family. He laughed a small Mister laugh that wrenched Jenny's heart. "Who knows? Maybe you'll be dirt poor, childless, and without any major responsibilities. I just want you to think about one thing. Just remember that already a little wait seems like too much to ask, that already every minute seems so important, that if you're waiting for something you want, waiting seems like an agony."

Jenny was catching on to Mister's line of reasoning. He was cutting deeply, about to touch the nerve that was now taut and vibrating in their own marital affairs.

"Now," Mister continued, "imagine that in a few years— let's even double your age—imagine that at that time you're

The Family Plan 117

saying to yourself, 'Okay, I have Peggy. We've been happy; we've had our ups and downs. I've been with her for half my natural life, and I stand a good chance of living enough years to constitute another lifetime.'" Mister took a tense breath as the incision hit its mark. "'Now what?' you ask yourself."

Jenny swallowed the anxious knot in her throat. She turned toward the books on Todd's dresser and absently thumbed through one on physics. Its binding was stiff and tough, and she finally understood the expression "crack the book." Todd's book spine hadn't been cracked. And he'll have the grades to prove it, too, she thought ruefully. Then he'd never get into college; he'd have so little to look forward to professionally. The situation was very serious, and Jenny was wise enough to know that the distractions would have to be dealt with. But not as Mister proposed.

She wanted to say something to offset what Mister was telling their son—she wanted to offer another side to the story—but she knew better. Mister was making a very solid point. And as much as it pained her, she had to let Todd hear it.

"What do you mean by, 'Now what?'" Todd asked.

"I mean that in starting your lifetime together so young, in diving headlong into this experience, you may be missing other opportunities, other paths," Mister said, his voice passionate. "You'll feel lacking, burdened by this one hasty choice!"

Jenny turned back to face her husband and son. Todd was not sitting pondering the great truths a masterful father had bestowed. He did not even seem to be considering them seriously. He was, in fact, looking slightly appalled.

"So?" he asked, shrugging his shoulders. "Do you think we can't grow together, that we can't work things out the way you and Mom have? Listen, Dad, you're the one who's always told me that life is a series of choices. That one choice is not necessarily better than the other, that the best thing I could ever do when in doubt is to trust my inner voice, to act in good faith, to follow my convictions." He got up and walked the length of the bed twice, shaking his head as he passed his father.

"Well, I really believe I'm living up to everything you two have ever taught me. I'm not worrying about something that might or might not happen in the future. I'm thinking about what I can do now. I'm thinking about what Peggy means to me, or what it would mean to me if we lost each other."

Todd stopped pacing to stand in front of Jenny. "What's the matter with you two?" he pleaded. "Are you losing your ideals? I can't believe how different you've been lately! I come to you, telling you that I've found the woman I want to spend my life with, and you pull something like this!"

Jenny reached for Todd's hand, and he impulsively turned to hug her, his tender shoulders quaking. "I love her, Mommy," he whispered. "I thought that was all that mattered to you and Daddy."

Jenny's hand cupped the back of her son's head. She hugged him and nodded into his shoulder. "It *is* all that matters, Todd."

Mister circled them, and Jenny felt that suddenly the odds had changed. Before, it had been two parents working on one idea for their son. Now, she felt, she and Todd were in an exclusive arena, and Mister stood outside it.

"What are you doing, Jenny?" he demanded, his voice low but firm. "I wish you'd leave it to me—"

"So that you can lecture me?" Todd interrupted.

Jenny tried to stop the wave of dissent she saw cresting, but Todd and Mister seemed to have their own inner reasons and workings propelling them.

"I'm your father," Mister began, "and I'm not going to let you make a foolish decision just because you feel strongly about it now. I can see the issues more clearly," he asserted. "You may think I'm being unreasonable," he struggled, "but I know what I'm doing. You and Peggy are *not* getting married. At least not now. I'm not asking you to wait, young man," Mister's low voice growled. "I'm *telling* you." He took a breath, as though it were settled.

"If you still feel this way next year, you can go ahead

and do whatever you want. But for now you're in my house, under my supervision, and subject to the rules here. And tomorrow, young man, you're going back to school!" Mister gave Jenny a backward glare, opened the door, and left Todd's room.

At first Todd looked pained and lost, as if he couldn't figure out what had gone wrong in a relationship that was normally open and compromising. Then, as he slowly pulled back from his mother, a light of comprehension lit his features. "He's talking about himself, isn't he, Mom?" he asked.

Jenny nodded, too emotional to answer lest she begin crying.

Todd hugged his mother and took a deep breath. "I didn't know," he marveled. "I thought you guys had the perfect thing going."

Jenny swallowed hard, hearing the workings of her brain resound through her head. "He's afraid history will repeat itself," she managed. "He didn't mean to come down on you that hard," she apologized self-consciously.

"That's okay," Todd assured her in a soft, concerned voice. "Because if there's one thing you two have taught me about life, it's to stick to your ideals. If he's lost his, I feel real bad, but I still believe in mine."

Jenny wanted to defend Mister; she wanted to explain that he still loved her and the family but that he felt trapped. And that that feeling was its own hell. But she knew her voice would not hold out that long.

"I'm just worried about you, Mommy," Todd's gentle voice intoned.

Jenny squeezed her lips together, closed her eyes, and breathed hard through her nose. The air passed the waiting tears and cooled them. She nodded, let her fingers brush her oldest child's arm, and resisted his entreaties to talk as she walked out of his room.

Downstairs, Mister was pouring himself a cup of coffee. Jenny gingerly skirted him as she withdrew the remains of the dinner from the warm oven, where Bea had left it for the absent family members.

Mister shook his head at it and then sat down across the

table from his wife. His eyes were moist.

"I honestly didn't realize just how affected you were by this discontent," Jenny whispered, not trusting herself to speak louder.

"I didn't know, either," Mister murmured. "I'm sorry."

Jenny sniffled and shrugged, rubbing her upper arms to ward off the emotional loneliness she felt. She had a lot of thoughts on the subject, but none was very well thought out. "It's a time bomb, you know," she said.

Mister shrugged this time. "It never exploded for you. Not yet, anyway."

"Somehow, for me, things are already getting better."

"You're very resilient," Mister complimented softly, both his hands wrapped around his hot coffee mug. "And very willing—".

"Are you willing to try something new for us, Mister? I mean, I feel a lot of changes happening around me in just these last few days. The reality of this house, the kids—everything has sort of changed for me. Maybe it's because Bea has suddenly taken over so many of the responsibilities. Maybe it's because for the first time I'm working." She tilted her head. "It's not the most demanding of jobs, I know, but for me, well, it's a big change."

She looked down at the platter of untouched food, glanced up the stairs, wondering about Todd, and then got up to put the dinner back into the oven. She leaned against the yellow counter top, and even the most familiar papers and children's paintings on the refrigerator looked alien to her.

"If you're not feeling the changes as much as I do," she mused softly, "maybe it's because the things you need changed haven't come to pass."

Mister looked up at his wife, their pained and loving eyes melding in a stare of long-standing love. "I'm willing," he told her, "but I don't know where to start."

"I want to say, 'Just look around, dummy', but I know it wouldn't matter. You see, even our showdown with Todd was reaffirming for me. He was defending love as the most important thing in life, and I remembered just how and why and when we felt the same thing toward each other. But you didn't see it that way."

Mister suddenly scraped his chair on the tile floor and stood up. He crossed to Jenny and held her in his arms. It was as though they'd never been close before. His heart was pounding against her breasts; his body seemed so firm, so new, so very, very warm.

He exhaled a choppy breath near her ear. "Help me, Jenny," he whispered in a voice so small she wasn't sure he trusted the sentiment. Then he turned his lips into her neck and said, "I want to see the things you're seeing. I want to say my reality within our marriage has changed, too. Help me, Jenny."

She held her husband's trembling body and heard him let out a sigh of anguish. "I intend to, Mister," she assured him. "I'm not letting you give up on us that easily."

But she knew that the lessons he had to learn would have to come slowly and with care. The last thing Jenny wanted was for her husband to feel rushed, manipulated. No, the changes couldn't be pointed out or described to him. He'd have to experience the strength, the love, the cure of their relationship firsthand.

She'd have to be very careful about this delicate point, and she was going to have to start by leading Mister to see that the life he craved—the one for which Heddy Lock was his consummate example and pioneer—was like any other existence in that it was not, in and of itself, magical. She had to let him notice that his idol was experiencing her own pain, her own crisis. That the freedom, the breathing room her life-style allowed meant relatively little to her in her situation. That the Heaths' household was happier, more at peace, than anything the Locks could make at this moment. Jenny had to make Mister understand that happiness and adventure were possible only when there was the security of mutual love. All else was a flat motion picture of gesturing jesters.

* * *

Jenny's first chance came the next morning, when, at the gallery, Mister poked his head into the back office where she and Heddy were sorting original prints.

"You know that old chest of drawers in the window?" he asked. "The one from France that you healed the other day?" Jenny recalled having rearranged the drawers so that the intricate veneer matched in the way the artisan had originally intended it to. "Two dealers before me, a restorer, Heddy, and I all thought it was supposed to be set the way it was. You right it, and guess what?"

Jenny shrugged her shoulders and turned her palms up.

Mister winked. "Give me the invoice pad," he directed Heddy. "Jenny just sold that piece. It's enough to pay for passage to Shanghai, for Pete's sake!"

There was a momentary celebration before the phone rang. Heddy followed Lloyd into the gallery. "Could you get that, Jenny?" she asked.

There was a strange clicking sound, and then the operator informed Jenny that it was China calling. "Wait, wait!" she exclaimed, recognizing the name of the important, out-of-the-way contact who was supposed to be getting Mister the Ming vases.

She ran into the gallery, but evidently Mister and Heddy had gone into the street to admire the piece with the buyer. She couldn't see them. They might even have gone to buy him a drink and to talk shop in the elegant Piper Pub.

She ran back to the phone and discovered that the caller spoke only rudimentary English. He was saying he couldn't get the vases, that they were—something she couldn't understand. Oh, where was Heddy, with her knowledge of Chinese? How in the world did anyone learn such a sing-song, intricate language?

She stayed on the phone, working up a sweat as she tried to convince the man to come across with the vases. She made a joke over not being able to communicate, and he began tittering. She spoke of everything she could think of that would keep them on equal ground. The man tried complimenting her, and they both laughed at the polite, sweet attempt.

The Family Plan

By the time Mister and Heddy had returned, Jenny was posing with a soapstone statue from India. Its eyes gazed heavenward, and its expressive hands reached out to the spectator. Heddy let out a laugh, and Mister pinched Jenny's bottom to get her to break her stance.

"Pleased with yourself, aren't you?" Mister commented, displaying the check for the chest of drawers.

"Sure am," she told the other two laconically. "But not because of *that* little sale. I got not one, not two, but *three* authentic Ming vases for a price so low you'll have to search the floor for it."

Excited, they got the details from her. Mister spun off to do a celebratory dance, then he swung over to his files and gave his wife a grin of appreciation as he pulled out a card. "Meticulous, aren't you?" he complimented. "You even filed the *M*'s under *M*."

"That's the way it's usually done," she remarked.

Heddy swaggered over to Jenny and whispered loudly enough for Mister to hear, "Not around here, it isn't."

"My wife's setting a good example," Mister said as he perused the file. "You were right about hiring her, Heddy." His gray eyes reflected the late morning sun. "However, I get the feeling you're conspiring to make a donkey out of me," he joked.

"Now, Lloyd," Jenny scolded in her best cowgirl accent, "you're the boss; I'm the hoss. But you might as well pay close attention. No telling what kind of lessons you'll learn." She delighted in the double meaning of her words. Already Mister might be seeing her in a different light. Already his perception of her and their possibilities together might be becoming more satisfying for him.

At noon, the three coworkers sat in the back office eating box lunches from the health bar. Jenny fed the baby the puréed vegetables she'd packed for his meal. The sun was shining in on him, and he was smiling and cooing at the adults. "I wonder what he's up to; he's not even pestering me to nurse," Jenny mused aloud.

"Try him," Mister suggested.

Jenny picked him up and set his kicking legs in her lap.

Automatically she freed her right breast and nuzzled it toward the baby's mouth. He looked the other way and smiled at Heddy.

"I can't believe it!" Jenny exclaimed. "None of my children ever did this. He's weaned himself! A week ago he would have learned to play 'The Minute Waltz' on a banjo if I'd offered him this opportunity. But now..." She stroked his velvety cheek to get him to face her. Heddy got out of her chair and squatted beside Jenny in the warm office that was slowly but surely being organized by the women's efficient hands.

"Maybe he's forgotten," Heddy offered, engrossed in the baby's reactions.

Jenny giggled. "Oh, you don't know babies. If there's one thing they never— There," she sighed as baby Lloyd nuzzled her nipple for a moment. Then, sputtering and laughing, he let it go and turned toward the window, where the colorful fall leaves swooshed against the glass.

"Odd," Jenny mused, laughing and tucking her bra back into place. She set the baby to crawl on the floor, and he made a beeline for his father.

She looked up, her avocado sandwich halfway to her mouth, and noticed Heddy's look of dismay.

Before she could ask anything, Heddy offered, "That *was* odd!" Jenny sensed she wasn't talking about the baby's refusal. "Oh dear, I'm in trouble now."

"What?" Jenny asked, adjusting her corduroy skirt and wedging off her elegant gray cowboy boots.

"Just now," Heddy began, "just now, watching you, I understood everything you've been saying about children. How they're terrible and wonderful, frustrating and satisfying. And," she said, an air of confidentiality in her whispery voice, "I understood what Paul's been saying, too."

"You mean his views on family life?" Mister put in, clearly interested in what Heddy had to say.

She nodded toward the couple. "He's forty. Forty! That's older than either of you, and look—you have six kids, while we haven't even begun!"

Mister chuckled softly. Both women looked at him. "Not everyone has to have children," he reminded her. "You and Paul might not even be happy with them."

"Of course I know that," Heddy responded. She leaned against the windowsill, appearing angelic and misty, the light diffused around her. Jenny's heart pounded as she quickly glanced to see if Mister had gotten the same impression. Obviously he had. His face was softened and opened toward the other woman. "But," Heddy continued, "I somehow feel I've been avoiding the issue."

"Maybe it's best that way, for you," Mister helped.

Heddy looked sideways, her profile exotic and dramatic against her flowing curtain of hair. "You mean career-wise?" Mister made a sound of agreement. "I love what I do," she assured them. "But sometimes I feel so—I don't know—like I have no motivation, like there's nothing and no one to do any of it for." Her sincere face turned toward them again, and Jenny intuited that this was the first time Heddy had ever admitted these feelings.

"It looks great from the outside. I work only when and if I want, I go where I please, I make a lot of money. But lately I've been turning down work." She addressed Lloyd. "I only took this job with you because I like you and had never worked in your gallery, and I wanted to be around a real, solid, good man. The kind of man who carries his family portrait around in a little Lucite frame, like the one you set up in hotel rooms, the kind of man who loves his wife and doesn't make passes at me, the kind who doesn't bluff his way through a sale like so many of our colleagues do..." She trailed off and gave a small smile to Jenny, who had quietly begun collecting the lunch wrappers.

Here was Jenny's chance to ask Heddy something she'd wondered about. "Do you love Paul?"

Heddy was toying with the buckle on her belt. She nodded. "I also loved my first husband, but I think I scared him off."

Mister gave a sweet, hearty laugh. "That must have been a job," he complimented.

Heddy smiled wanly and furrowed her dark eyebrows. "I was so adamant about not committing myself to anyone that he made another commitment."

"Well, you can't become what someone else expects," Mister defended.

"I could have worked with him. Compromised. The way you and Jenny do."

"It's not always easy!" Jenny exclaimed.

"But you *do* it. Making room in my life for other people is not among my best skills. And then I see you, Jenny, handling emergencies with the kids, relating to Lloyd, flowing right into his work, and I feel so—I don't know—inadequate."

Jenny let out a guffaw as she bent to scoop up the baby before he had the chance to topple a pile of boxes onto himself. "The ultimate irony!" she hooted. "I look at your life and feel the same way!"

"You're both extraordinary," Mister put in. "It's a common human tendency to look into greener pastures and envy..." He trailed off and gave a small shrug and an enigmatic smile. Good! Jenny thought. He was getting the picture. She'd always known that any life was only as good as the happiness it brought.

"Is it serious?" Jenny began. "I mean with Paul here in Piper and waiting for you to decide between him and a career?"

Heddy nodded.

"He's entertaining some pretty staunch opinions," Mister said.

"I can't get *him* to see that. I think he feels he has to be so starchy because I'm so thick-headed!"

Jenny engaged Heddy's glance before she teased, "I think it was very intelligent of you—marrying a man because his work suited your schedule."

"Think you're cute, don't you?" Heddy asked, her hazel eyes dancing with fond amusement.

"I'm as cute as you're smart," Jenny quipped. "It's real drudgery to marry for love, you know. It makes you make all kinds of sticky sacrifices that under normal circumstances would certify you as insane." She winked at Mister.

"I'm not much of a martyr myself," Heddy retorted, obviously repressing a smile.

"Why did you marry a man like Paul?" Jenny hedged. "You must have known he was such an—I don't know— such an earthy man before you agreed to the match."

Jenny could tell that she was on to something, that she was touching on a point that both Heddy and Mister needed to hear for their respective problems. Heddy turned to face the small yard beyond the back alley. Her face looked soft yet fixed in the bright noon sun. "You two could tell that about him, couldn't you?"

Mister answered. "He wasn't quite what we expected."

"I don't know why I fell in love with a man like Paul."

Jenny smiled and told Heddy something she often told her children. "You do know why. We set ourselves up so that we get what we ask for in life." She went to stand near the other woman. "He's probably your complement, your mate. You probably need the things he could show you." She paused dramatically and grimaced comically at Heddy. *"After* you've fought out all the problems."

"Everybody fights. In the end, if your love—your relationship—is strong, you find that the other person has helped you become the person you always wanted to be but couldn't be alone."

Heddy smiled a deep, womanly smile. "That's a romantic notion, Guinevere Heath!"

"It sure is, Heddy Lock." Then Jenny smiled, too. "What are you going to do?"

"He says if I go to China with Lloyd, he won't be waiting for me when I get back."

"Are you coming?" Mister wanted to know.

"I'll see," Heddy responded. "I'll see."

The lunch was cleared away, the conversation done, and a lot of quiet work awaited them. As Jenny meticulously catalogued each print by title, artist, year, medium, number in the edition, and provenance, she wondered if Mister was slowly realizing that a life he'd admired was not all he'd imagined it to be. Sure, the one he'd made with her had its built-in problems. Sure, he felt trapped by those problems and by his youthful decisions. He'd made that clear to her in their private conversations, in their dinner debate with the Locks, and especially through his stern, almost obsessive, lecture to Todd.

But did he see that all around him were the flying sparks of two new developments—steps that might help him keep what he loved while he grew and branched out? For one thing, the very structure of the Heath household was evolving at a tremendously accelerated rate. Never before had so much transpired in such essential ways in such a short period of time.

There was even a new breed of problem in their household. And Todd's was going to be the first in a long line of more adult issues and questions to be dealt with.

The knowledge of this new phase was both thrilling and unnerving to Jenny. It meant that their family was entering another growth period—that their children were maturing, that they were soon going to be making that leap into the wilds of the outer world, leaving the family nest.

Already Karen and Joyce were aware of what lay beyond sibling relationships; already Matthew was forming a sense of his own independence; and already Amy was forming ties outside the home. It would be a rough road, but it eventually would free the Heath parents. Jenny hoped Mister was coming to recognize this.

The other development in Jenny's and Mister's life involved their blossoming friendship with the Locks. Here was the example of a possible other life staring them right in the face. Of course it was only one of infinite possibilities, but for Jenny and Mister, there could hardly have been a more perfectly set-up contrast. Heddy and Paul had married late, worked apart, endured long absenses from each other, and had no children or home they were responsible for. And Heddy's career was the kind Mister had often coveted—the kind that had been denied him by virtue of his familial duties.

The Family Plan 129

Jenny was willing to endure anything with Mister. If he could just see the freedom they were beginning to have, their horizons would be limitless! She respected his right to doubt; she admired his analytical processes. But his constant support of Heddy was nerve-racking. It was only a matter of time before he saw what Jenny was seeing—if he was willing to look closely at all.

9

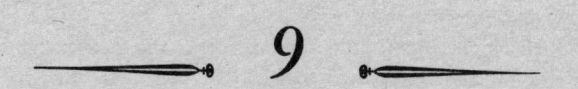

IT WAS SUNDAY, one of those magical days that heralded the transformation of one season into another. Within the last week, since Jenny had met the Locks, the fall leaves had been raining down like incessant precipitation. The air had been losing some of its summer warmth, and today it took on the delicious, crisp chill of autumn.

As Jenny dressed for a brunch to which the children had invited their parents and the Locks, she felt a giddiness welling up in the depths of her chest. She'd been so involved in her own concerns and her new life at the gallery that she'd let her home life take a back seat while she sped away into the heavy traffic of change and self-absorption. One part of her was tingly with excitement, as though she were the honored guest at a celebratory function, but another part of her was frightened to death.

Her palms were damp with nervous perspiration as she tried to work the tiny pearl buttons that went from wrist to elbow on her otherwise flouncy cashmere and angora sweater. Her life was in such transition. Todd was set on marrying.

Marrying! Baby Lloyd had, very painlessly and capably, weaned himself. Matthew had bitten a hefty chunk out of the process called growing up. The girls had become so independent and competent that they had even organized this very grown-up affair. Bea was taking charge where Jenny had left off, and Mister...

Well, Jenny ruminated as she twisted the pale green wool skirt around her hips, Mister was on the verge of a breakthrough.

She went to the full-length mirror in the bathroom to check her appearance. The deep hunter-green blousy sweater, the pale green skirt, the delicate sling-back beige heels all looked sleek and flattering. It was her vulnerable face that needed a dressing up.

Her blond brows knitted in dismay as she faced the horrible truth. She'd always primed her family for independence. Now that they seemed not only capable of it but comfortable with it, a heavy stone caught in her throat. In doing such a good job, she'd created her own monster. She swept a weary hand through her hair as she named the beast. She called it Loneliness, she called it Planned Obsolescence, she called it Mud, and she wondered if her name-baby books had an appropriate first name for it—because whatever the creature was called, she was going to have to get on a first-name basis with it.

She wet a cosmetics sponge and worked a peachy foundation into it. As she applied the makeup, she fought the welling sorrow that threatened to defy her resolve.

"Stop feeling so sorry for yourself!" she commanded. "It's degrading. You always expected the children to grow up." The mirror suddenly moved, signaling that someone was behind the door. Jenny put her hand to her mouth, as if it had been speaking without her consent.

She poked her head around to see who was there and was relieved to be looking down into baby Lloyd's cute little face. He gave her a dopey, sleepy grin. She picked him up and squeezed his chubby body to herself, feeling the firmness of his eager arms and reveling in his delighted squawk.

"Getting around on your own these days, eh, kid?" she teased, tweaking his tiny, pudgy nose. The baby rubbed his eyes with his fat fists and gave his mother one of those innocent, completely open smiles only children and ancient mystics could manage.

"You think I'm okay, don't you, little guy?" she asked him as she sat him on the sink and wedged him safely between her stomach and the wall. She used the mirror above the sink to finish applying her makeup. "You still need me, don't you?" She brushed her blusher on with soft, light strokes. "And someday you might even think I'm pretty nice. You might tell me your problems like the rest do. You might come to me knowing that I'll accept and love you no matter what—the way Todd does."

She stopped fluttering her mascara wand and stared at the baby who seemed very interested in her monologue. She touched his soft cheek with the back of her hand. "You can't fool me with those puppy eyes," she whispered. "Someday you'll leave, too."

Jenny finished with the mascara and gently set the baby on the tiled bathroom floor that had never seen cleaner days since Bea's arrival. She slowly shook out her curly hair and bent over to run her fingers through it in final preparation for the family brunch.

She didn't want it to happen—she didn't want the ache in her chest to throb this way; she didn't want to drip tears on Bea's meticulous floor—but it happened anyway. Oh, damn that man, she cried to herself. Why can't he just be less thorough for once? Why can't he just live with his unhappiness like the rest of us do?

She laughed at herself through her tears and raised her head in ironic mirth. Since that lunchtime talk at the gallery, Mister hadn't come to the startling conclusions she had. Nor had the conversation with Todd changed his views.

She'd always expected to lose the children. She'd even half expected to go through life wondering what she'd missed. But she'd never expected to lose her Mister. She swiped at a persistent tear. She'd never expected to feel like this— alone, his precious love uncertain, their complete and mutual understanding layered over with a coat of offensive varnish that yellowed and cracked the brilliance of their idyllic life together, the way it damaged precious old paintings.

Making herself presentable again, she tossed her head, coaxed the baby out of the bathroom by walking his crawling body between her feet, and snickered. Well, she thought, taking a deep breath and sighing, at least her metaphors were changing. She wasn't "just a mother and housewife" anymore. All her ambitions were seeing the light of the day after years of preparation in the dark. All of the things she'd worked for were now working for her. Except the most important, her reason for even living—Mister Lloyd Heath.

She was facing the most fundamental conflict of her life, and she was facing it, essentially, alone.

She maneuvered the baby into the hallway and stopped short at the sight of Mister and Heddy, silhouetted against the semicircular alcove of frosted glass and padded window seats. They were talking earnestly, their heads bent together. Mister seemed to have that air of mastery about him, that sober confidence Jenny always found so attractive.

Jenny clutched at her heart and quickly retreated back into the safety of her room. Baby Lloyd plopped onto the floor outside her open door and waved gleefully at his mother. "Shh!" she whispered, her thoughts colliding like speeding railway cars attached to an engine that had hit a wall. Keep it in perspective, she reprimanded herself. After all, they've been friends for a long time.

Then Mister's voice called out, "Jenny?" She heard him mumble something about the baby's being alone. She gulped down the hard stone of fear in her throat and assumed a nonchalant air as she stepped into the hallway and whisked up the baby. Pretending she couldn't possibly have noticed the couple because she was so involved in being a mommy, she made cooing sounds that sounded strained even in her own pounding ears.

"Oh, there you are," Mister said. Where had he been looking for her? Jenny wondered. In Heddy's eyes? "Heddy

The Family Plan

and Paul are here, and I was just bringing Heddy up to use our bathroom and to find you."

Jenny glided forward, aware of her friend's eyes, which seemed to convey a desperate fervor to talk.

"We'll be down in a minute," Jenny told Mister. "Tell the others, won't you?" She gestured for Heddy to enter the bedroom and pointed out the bathroom.

Mister waited for the other woman to cross the carpeted room before he spoke into Jenny's ear. "You look delicious," he said, sexual insinuation coloring his tone. Then—impulsively, Jenny guessed—he grabbed her and fit his lips over hers.

Her breath was taken away by the surprising force of his embrace. He sucked on her tongue and wrestled his straining lips on hers, crushing both their mouths in a rotating, gyrating fashion.

Just as abruptly he pulled away, murmuring, "Hurry down."

"Who were you kissing, Mister?" Jenny whispered, her voice choked and small. "Me or the one you can't touch?"

She shouldn't have said it. Mister's eyes were disbelieving and hurt. But still, she'd been feeling so unsure, so afraid and lost. "If you don't know," Mister murmured, "I can't tell you." He took the baby and hurried down the hall.

Jenny bit her fist and closed the door of her bedroom.

Heddy immediately appeared at the bathroom door, clearly in a rush to say something. Gliding over to Jenny, she sat on the vanity seat, her face bright and animated. "My period's two days late," she confided.

A gasp caught in Jenny's throat. "Could be anything," she ventured.

Heddy raised her black eyebrows. "I don't really know. I'm always regular, but with Paul's new demands and the trip zooming up on me..." Her eyes seemed filled with both anticipation and a certain soft, fearful moisture.

"Bea, our housekeeper, says, *'Che sarong, sarong!'* " Jenny said with a smile. "It's too early to tell."

"I don't *feel* different."

They started out of the room, but Heddy grabbed Jenny's arm. "You won't say anything to the men."

Jenny chuckled softly, the sound originating deep in her throat, where it seemed the emotions of the whole morning had been residing.

Heddy shook her head quickly, apologetically. "That was stupid. Of course you wouldn't."

It was obvious to Jenny that if Heddy had been sensing anything from Mister, she was doing a good job of not letting herself believe it. "Lloyd was showing me the collection you two have made. I hope you're heavily insured," she exclaimed, complimenting the Heath's decor.

"Not enough," Jenny muttered as the two women reached the dining room. "We've never had enough insurance." Against catastrophes and surprises, she added silently.

The children were proud of what they'd done, and justly so. Jenny's summery patterned china was arranged in light, airy place settings at the table. There was a centerpiece of fruits, ferns, and flowers. The serving pieces from the large china set were brimming with steaming selections.

Todd pulled out a chair for Heddy and then went around the table to seat his mother and Bea. Paul, who looked gorgeous in his turtleneck sweater, soft corduroy jacket, and worn jeans, helped Joyce and Karen, who took their places with all the grace and charm of worldly women. Jenny smiled as she caught their secretly exchanged "Wow!" glance over Paul's looks. When Paul seated Amy, she reached up, signaled for him to come closer, and then kissed him on the cheek. Everyone at the table began laughing as Amy, not even blushing, took a head bow.

The brunch *would* have to start with a bang, Jenny thought as Matthew, who had seated himself, spouted, "Stop being such a show-off in front of Mommy and Daddy's friends, Amy."

Amy wrinkled her nose impertinently at her brother, then gave a gracious nod of acknowledgment toward the Locks.

Jenny burst out laughing and told Mister, "She looks

The Family Plan

more like Miriam every day!"

"Oh, I admire Aunt Miriam greatly," Amy emoted.

"Had we known that in advance, little lady," Mister responded, taking up her gracious nodding, "we would have named you for her."

"Oh, no," Jenny put in. "Miriam is a derivative of Mary: bitter." She shook her head. "That would never do."

"For whom was I named, Mother?" Karen's lyrical voice asked.

Jenny smiled. "For yourself. Pure. And Joyce is joyful."

"I wasn't named for anybody," Matthew observed. "I'm just God's gift." He gave a pixie grin and wrinkled his stubby nose.

Amy moaned. "God's gift to tarantulas and all the reptilian creatures of the earth, you mean."

Heddy and Paul Lock burst into pealing laughter over this.

"I wish Mommy would sew a sack over your face," Matthew told his sister. "You're so ugly my eyes hurt when I have to look at you!"

Amy must have forgotten her extraordinary manners, for she stood up, her still-sewed lip quivering, and shot Matthew an arresting glare.

"She can't wait to get her stitches out so that she can start kissing that boy at school again," Matthew continued. He inclined his head toward the Locks and told them, "They're going to make a baby if they don't watch it!"

This started an uproar of laughter, rebuttals, confusion, and blushes around the table.

Finally Bea Kirke stood up, pounded the table once with her fist, and sat down again, this time to a hushed shock. "Mealtimes are for chowing down," she observed philosophically as she eyed the assembled company. "And I don't mean on each other."

Joyce and Karen let out embarrassed laughs. Jenny was definitely going to have a talk with them—she suspected they were going through that horrible tyranny of the hormones that tainted every word with sexual innuendo. They giggled so much! Well, at least she was consoled by the fact that they saw humor in sex; that would help them later on.

Amy's quivering lip shuddered, then she quickly left the table, calling, "Mommy!" as she went. Jenny excused herself and took up pursuit. She ended up on the den couch with her young daughter halfway in her lap.

She listened to her daughter's plaints, answering her questions about boys, until Amy, refreshed and relieved, suggested they go back to their party.

Everyone in the dining room was talking at once, enjoying each other's company and exchanging ideas that flew helter-skelter among the adults and children. Amy immediately caught the drift of something Heddy and Todd were discussing, and Jenny settled in to enjoy the banter and her breakfast.

The doorbell rang, and Todd cut off his talk to run to get it. By the way he glanced at his mother, she felt a certain suspicion about the identity of the caller.

Paul was saying, "Oh, Jenny, I really admire you and Lloyd. What a great bunch of kids you have!" His eyes shone with merriness, and Jenny could tell that Paul Lock was a man made for family life. She held the secret of Heddy's possible pregnancy like a precious seed in her heart, wishing the Locks a lifetime of the familial happiness she and Mister had known.

Heddy was telling the girls what a good job Jenny was doing at the gallery. "I've become a useless appendage," she stated. "Or, really, your mother's assistant!"

"Your mother's a natural out there," Mister agreed. "Soon she won't need any of us."

"Oh, we'll all always need each other," Jenny returned meaningfully. "Even if for different reasons."

Jenny didn't know who stopped talking first, but in the sudden silence she turned around to see Todd. Peggy was standing beside him, her fresh young face flushed and pretty. Todd made quiet introductions.

"Hi, Mrs. Heath," Peggy said, bending swiftly to place

The Family Plan

a nervous, sweet kiss on Jenny's cheek. "I really fell for it that time in the restaurant. Even when Todd told me who you really were, I could hardly believe it. You're so young!"

Jenny smiled and glanced at Mister, who was already getting Peggy a chair. There was a tangible tension in the room as everyone tried to figure out everyone else's relationship to each other. Only Karen, who gave a small wave and smile to Peggy, exposed the fact that Todd had probably confided in her at one time or another about his special relationship with Peggy.

After a few moments of awkwardness, the party picked up its tempo again, and Peggy, her shy, young eyes plainly eager for anything this family would share with her, took it all in with reddened cheeks but apparent grace.

"I see what he sees in her," Jenny confided to Mister as they went into the kitchen together to refill the coffee pot.

Mister gave her a sidelong glance. "She reminds me of you at that age."

"Oh, I was never that self-conscious," she defended.

Mister winked at her. "Think again," he advised. "It's uncanny how similar you were to her."

When they returned to the table, Bea excused herself to go catch a bus out to her son's house, where, she said, she was going to have to make room for some real food. They all joked over Jenny's unorthodox diet for her family, but she had their health, happiness, and good spirits to point to as a measure of success.

"And look, Ma," Todd teased, "no cavities!"

Jenny wouldn't hear of letting Bea stay to help clean up. She walked her to the door, sending her on her way with a hug and a kiss of gratitude. "Oh don't thank me, Jenny girl," Bea said. "You're the one who set them all straight. I just sort of,"—she turned an imaginary button in the air—"put them into motion. The rest is stuff they learned from you and your husband." Then she hugged Jenny again. "Do some more fighting," she advised, seemingly out of the blue. "He needs a good swift kick in his historical background before he'll appreciate what he's got."

Jenny laughed and tapped Bea on her own well-endowed background. "Beatrice," she said pensively. "She who brings joy." She looked into the other woman's eyes and teased, "It'll do."

When Jenny returned to the dining room, Heddy had a large glass of water in her hand and was fighting off the baby, who seemed to want to gobble it all down in one gulp. "Help!" she cried as Jenny appeared. "I'm afraid of this kid!"

"Don't be," Mister advised, visibly enjoying Heddy's plight. "He catches on quick. He'll tryannize you."

"Better you than me," Jenny ribbed her friend.

Heddy let out a groan, and the more her husband jostled her, teasing her about the baby, the louder her groans got.

"Come on, Heddy," Mister said, getting up and nodding all around. "I'll show you the stuff we didn't get a chance to look at before."

Gratefully she relinquished baby Lloyd, took Mister's hand, and stood up, casting a beautiful backward glance to Jenny and Paul with her magnetic hazel eyes.

Jenny gave her a smile, but a fierce fear pounded in her chest. Her heart began furiously pumping blood through her system, advising her to take flight or to fight. Paul must have noticed it because he made a show of getting up to stretch. She left the kids and led Paul into the den, where she selected an album of early jazz singers and turned the stereo on low.

She sat across from Paul, on the low ottoman, while he stretched his large body out on the carpet. "I like your children," he said.

"I've gotten used to them," Jenny observed, trying to smile at her own wit.

"It must have taken a tremendous team to build them into what they are today."

Overhead, Jenny heard the creaking of an old floorboard, and she knew that Mister and Heddy were now in Matthew's room. Her eyes darted involuntarily upward. Matthew had never figured out how his parents could guess so uncannily

The Family Plan

the times he was up and about after hours.

Paul's eyes shot up, following Jenny's. "She doesn't know," he confided.

"I've been wondering if it would make a difference in the course of events if she did," Jenny said with a sigh.

Paul shrugged and watched her intently. "Hey," he coaxed, leaning his formidable body forward and taking hold of Jenny's perspiring hand. "Don't be so worried. They've been alone plenty of times before, and nothing's ever happened."

Jenny looked nervously upward again as she heard a gentle creaking that suggested that the two people upstairs weren't walking, but maybe rocking. She tried to imagine them, studious and intent, leaning over the bronze statue that stood on Matthew's desk. Instead, she got a mental image of the way Mister sometimes held her and rocked her seductively in his arms.

Jenny winced at the thought that Mister had been confiding his feelings to Heddy at that window in the hallway before. She closed her eyes and prayed that he hadn't expressed himself then, and that he wasn't doing so now.

"Heddy says you're primed enough to go on the China trip," Paul was saying.

Jenny gave a distracted smile and nodded absently.

His eyes followed her thoughts upward as the floorboards creaked again, this time signaling that the pair upstairs was moving on. Paul Lock had clever, bright eyes, Jenny noticed. He seemed like a man of wisdom and strength. "Why don't you go?" he asked.

"To China?" Jenny responded.

He nodded, and Jenny saw that he really was a fast thinker. "That would solve some problems, don't you think?" he queried.

Jenny drew her attention to the man and gave a sigh of resignation tinged with humor. She shook her head, smiling at him. "I know that your taking that particular course of action—forcing Heddy to see you night and day in a new light—has been working for you two," she began, letting her other hand join their clasped ones to make a friendly, comradely hand sandwich. "But throwing myself at Mister's toes and begging for clemency won't help me. I'm not a woman who has custody of her wiles. What Lloyd needs is something I needed."

"What's that?" Paul asked, knitting his eyebrows in interest.

"I don't need him to be noble or to stay with me because of our family, or to simply take out a new lease on this old, mortgaged life of ours. His doubts would just be perpetuated, Paul. He would have solved nothing of his real problem."

She let go of Paul's hands, stood up, and began pacing the room—something she always did when her thoughts seemed out of control. Her eyes met Paul's. "He's been the faithful Schnauzer long enough. He obeys reason, not impulse. But those impulses, those secret wishes—whether they involve Heddy or just what she represents to him—all those ugly, seething monsters that are keeping him from me now will surface again if they're not put to rest!"

Still pacing, she continued, "You see, since Heddy came into our lives, mine has changed drastically. I'm a different person to my children; the house and I are no longer in a love-hate affair; I feel confident—after that China deal, you know, the one involving the vases?"

Paul nodded; evidently, Heddy had told him about the incident.

"I have Bea living with us now. The baby's all weaned, and I feel, well, I feel that life has really and truly changed for me."

"I understand," Paul said, running a finger over his moustache and listening, Jenny could tell, to every sound from above. "I somehow couldn't imagine that the problem was a common marital one between you two. It's more of a set of personal crises, isn't it? Like the one I could soon be experiencing if Heddy decides against me."

"Oh, she won't," Jenny assured him. "Trust my instincts—they're seldom wrong." She could not betray what

The Family Plan

Heddy had confided. Even though it might help allay Paul's doubts and even help his marriage, she was under a womanly pledge of honor to leave the unfolding of the Locks' events to their own devices.

The conversation effectively at a standstill, the two headed back toward the dining room.

Jenny stopped at the foot of the stairs to listen for Heddy and Mister. Todd appeared and put his arm around her shoulder, leading her into the kitchen, where Peggy was standing, her knuckles against her front teeth.

"What is it?" Jenny asked them.

"Do you think Pop will ever forgive us?" Todd blurted as he put an arm around Peggy's waist. "He was so mad that day in my room—as if I were doing something deliberately to hurt him."

Jenny gazed at the young couple and put a tender hand on each of their shoulders. Smiling at Peggy, she mused, "The pearl." Then she looked into their young and hopeful eyes set in faces that so reminded her of her own love life's past. "If I thought I had any hope of dissuading you..." she began before trailing off in silent self-reproach at her preaching.

She touched her son's face and felt its soft stubble that she knew would soon grow to approximate his father's scratchy mass. "Go into this with one thought in mind," she advised, her waiting tears rebelling and falling. As she wiped them she complained, "God! Is growing up always so hard for us? I feel like I've been hooked up to heaven's water main lately!"

Peggy giggled and smiled softly. "I'm always crying, too," she sympathized.

"Yes, but you're supposed to. You're at the most volatile age of your life." She gave a tiny chuckle, knowing that she, too, was facing one of life's transitions.

"What thought, Mom?" Todd prodded, his eyes begging for words of wisdom.

"The most important thing to nurture is your love for each other. In the end, that's all that will matter. It'll be the one thing to sustain you throughout life."

How painful it was to give the very advice she so believed in but could not be sure of for herself right now—unless Mister was awakening to the very revelations she'd been having. Unless the events of their topsy-turvy life were coalescing into an intelligible affirmation of their relationship for him.

Jenny saw the burning in Todd's and Peggy's eyes, the sweet enthusiasm over life and love, the inspiration fueled by their ideals, and she couldn't bear to warn them of trials that as yet had no weight in love's measure.

"I love you, Mommy," Todd said as he embraced her impulsively.

"I love you, too," Peggy whispered as she joined the huddle. Tears welled in her tender eyes. "Todd's told me so much about you, I truly feel I already know you," she managed. "And what I've already seen, I already love."

Jenny smiled wistfully and followed them to the door, giving them each a tight hug before they scooted down the driveway to Peggy's waiting car.

Mister and Heddy were already in the dining room when Jenny went in. She took the baby from Paul, who had also returned and was quietly bouncing the infant on his knee. She sat down next to Matthew, falling with blessed relief into a conversation about fruit trees and gardens.

Everyone in her family was changing, it was true, but the fear and nervousness she'd felt while dressing this morning were gone, replaced by the sure knowledge that she was not obsolete to her family—that she was merely changing along with them, offering them the things they needed for their particular phases of growth.

She looked at her changing family with new eyes, with renewed hope, and with a certain strength that she could accept anything from any of them.

Didn't Mister feel the thrill of their evolution? Didn't he see the perfect opportunities for reaffirmation and growth?

Karen sidled over to Jenny and whispered a request. "I'm

supposed to give a speech in class tomorrow," she began. "I want you to hear it."

Jenny pulled back to smile at her daughter. "Sure."

Karen bit her lower lip, which was tinted with a soft pink lipgloss, and said tentatively, "I'd like to practice it in front of everyone."

Jenny made the arrangements, and soon the Locks and the Heaths were listening to Karen's soft, lyrical voice tell the story of her choosing—the story of her family.

"My family is the closest, happiest, most understanding in the world," she began in a timid but determined voice. "Nothing beats being around them—not even coming to school—because in my family, no one would ever tell me to get up and make a speech like this. No one would ever expect me to be anybody other than who I am. No one would ever force their demands on me, or force me to prove myself.

"My mother is so good that you'd think I was bragging if I told you even one of the nice things about her.

"My father isn't like other fathers, who growl and cuss at their supposed love ones—"

Mister cleared his throat, and Karen stopped talking. "Sounds like you've got a bit of a chip on your shoulder about the world at large, young lady," he observed. "Are you sure you want to give that kind of speech?"

"I'm sure," Karen told her father. "Because it's all true. There's nothing like being a part of this family," she said. "Out there everyone wants you to be just like them. I resent that. Here at home, with my parents and brothers and sisters, everyone gets to be exactly who they are, and that's a bigger deal than the rest of you think. People who are quiet, like me, feel those pressures the most."

Mister nodded his approval, and Karen gave a big smile that grew progressively wider as she went on with her talk.

When Jenny and Mister caught each other's eyes, they shook their heads familiarly and exchanged warm smiles of love and rueful dismay.

Mister hunched down to slink around the others and

hunker close to Jenny and baby Lloyd. He rested his hand possessively on Jenny's knee.

"She's really quite brave," he whispered, his eyes bright and intent on their shy daughter. Oh, how Jenny wished he'd say something reassuring about their relationship. She wanted to shake him out of his problems and then kiss him all over.

Jenny squeezed her lips together and nodded tightly, a lump of pride caught in her throat. "She's an okay kid," she managed as Karen finished her speech.

Everyone stood up to applaud Karen. Mister squatted again, taking the baby into his lap. With an electric bolt, his gray eyes connected with Jenny's. "You've been a great mother," he said, reaching out momentarily to stroke Karen's arm as she passed.

"We've both done our duty to them," Jenny murmured meaningfully, her eyes still held by his. For the first time, she was aware that he was actually beginning to see their situation in a new light.

She was aware, too, that the knowledge of their family's self-sufficiency might backfire, bringing not the realizations she'd hoped for, but a sense of relief for Mister. He might just as easily decide it was the safest moment to leave her as he would decide it was the most promising of times together yet.

She nodded and averted her eyes a bit shyly. Chuckling, Mister lifted her chin with his index finger. "See? You are like Todd's Peggy. I remember when a blush was a permanent rouge on your cheeks."

Jenny gave a tender smile. The din of activity around them receded, leaving the two of them acutely aware of each other. "It's been a joy and a strain these years," she said. Mister smiled softly, touching a flyaway fluff of wool on her sweater. "Have you been staying lately out of a sense of duty?" Jenny asked softly.

Mister looked incredulous. "Have you?" he returned, a bit wickedly, Jenny thought.

"You know better than that," she admonished. "But what's

The Family Plan

to hold us together after all these torrid confessions of discontent?" she half teased.

Jenny always saw Mister as being the same young man she'd fallen in love with so many years ago. Now his handsome face furrowed into a frown that made him appear as he seldom did—older, more mature, accomplished, and very sexy. "If everything else is going or gone," he reasoned, "then all that's left is you and me."

"Until the bitter end?" Jenny mused, her voice a hush of fear and wonder.

"It'd better not be." Mister winked. "It'd better not be!"

10

THE FALL CHILL billowed the curtains of the dining room. Jenny and Mister had ended up there after the Locks had left for the Lady K, Joyce and Karen had gone off roller skating with friends from the show at school, Matthew had gone to dinner and a video-recorded movie at his friend's house, and Amy had begged to sleep overnight at her best schoolmate's.

Jenny tidied her pile of the Sunday paper and got up to close the windows. She rubbed her upper arms. "It really smells like winter's coming on out there."

Mister looked up from the arts section and gave her a small smile. Then, as she took her place at the oak refectory table again, he leaned his chin against his palm and stared at her.

Jenny felt his eyes like two hot fingers on her downcast eyelids, and she lifted her gaze. Mister looked so pensive, so quietly reflective. She smiled at her husband, and with her thumb and forefinger she rubbed the edges of her lipsticked mouth. She cleared her throat. "What are you staring at?" she asked.

"You," came the quiet reply.

"Why?" She almost wrung her hands, but instead she gathered the news section and arranged it back into its original folds—a feat she seldom achieved.

"We're all alone," he reminded her.

"Baby Lloyd's asleep on the couch," she pointed out.

"He won't tell," Mister slurred, a lazy grin playing on his sexy mouth. "He's a trustworthy boy."

Jenny looked at her hands, which were foolishly clasped on the pile of newspapers before her. She bit her bottom lip as she wondered what would happen to Mister's relationship with the children if he ever decided to leave her. "What did you and Heddy talk about?" she asked.

"Our collection..." He seemed to be leaving the sentence unfinished.

"And?"

"And?" Mister repeated, sighing and reaching across to take his wife's hand. "And the trip."

"That's all?" She remembered Heddy's eyes after she and Mister had been in the hallway alcove.

"That's all," he answered. "I told you I wouldn't exclude you if I ever decided to have a more revealing chat with her. I'd talk to you about it first." He got up and stood behind Jenny, gently rubbing her tense shoulders.

"Are you planning to? I mean, do you intend to have that chat?"

He dug his fingers seductively into her shoulders and answered, "That would be futile at this point. I'd have nothing revealing to say."

Jenny reached up to pat her husband's hand. She rotated in her seat and looked at his solemn but alluring gray eyes. Her head cocked to one side, she asked, "Do you still feel attracted to her?"

"It's changing," Mister answered, his eyes clouding, seeming to look into his thoughts. He got down on his knees next to her and took Jenny's right foot in both his hands. Removing her beige sling-backs, he began rubbing her toes. "I'm beginning to see that I was wrong about Paul."

The Family Plan

"Oh?" Jenny answered, her foot tensing.

Mister worked the flat of his thumbs on the ball of her foot. "By the way she'd always behaved so independently of him, I had assumed that he wasn't a very nice man."

Jenny let out a small moan as Mister's thumbs dipped into the arch of her foot, her slippery pantyhose slithering suggestively over her skin. "He adores her, you know," she told Mister. "But that's not to say you can't still feel what you feel for Heddy."

Mister worked her heel between his strong fingers, making her entire foot and all its corresponding points in her body feel aflame. "Attraction is not love, my dear girl," he told his wife as he sat back, flicked off her other shoe, and nestled the second foot in his lap. "I never said I was in love with her."

Jenny gave a throaty laugh. "And a good thing, too!" she exclaimed, "because if you were, you'd be sleeping alone. At least you'd be sleeping without me."

Mister cradled Jenny's foot and got up onto his knees again. He sent his gray gaze deep into her soul. "I don't want to sleep without you," he whispered, making Jenny's skin feel alive with tiny magnetized hairs. "And I wish I had never expressed any of this damn business to you."

"Keep the wife in the dark, eh?" Jenny asked, her swelling heart knowing that Mister would never be able to hide from her for very long.

"No, I like a little light on," he insinuated sexily.

Suddenly she was afraid of talking to Mister, afraid of hearing too much about his feelings toward a woman she'd come to respect, admire, and care about. She was afraid to be Mister's confessor in something that so deeply involved her, her very life, her now-precarious future.

Jenny pulled her foot from Mister's grasp and stood up. He reached for her, but she only smiled tensely and walked briskly to the kitchen, where she began emptying the dishwasher of her good china. She needed time alone, time to think.

Mister was leaning against the doorjamb, tapping a pencil

against his big, beautiful teeth. "Leave those," he told her. "I want to talk to you some more."

Jenny had her back to him. "Then talk," she suggested, her heart working double time.

The baby often picked bad times to awaken, but as Jenny heard his wail she dried her hands on an apron hanging on the refrigerator door and ran to him. "Mommy's here, baby!" she called. "I'm coming!"

She passed Mister on her way to change the baby in the bathroom and gave him a practiced look of preoccupation. No talk, her thoughts warned. No talk!

On the pretense of nursing baby Lloyd, Jenny retreated to the bedroom, where she and he fell asleep in the dark.

Some hours later, Mister woke her with a kiss on her sleep-softened lips. His eyes were bright in the moonlight of the cold, cloudless night. Instinctively Jenny reached up and hugged her husband. Then she sat up in bed. "Mmm." She stretched. "You're still dressed. Did you sleep?" She felt better now, having had a beautiful dream that replayed their conversation during Karen's speech. Somehow it had satisfied and warmed her with hope.

Mister's voice was soft. "I fell out on the couch in the den."

"Are they all home?" Jenny asked.

Mister nodded. "It was Bea who got me up so that she could watch an old movie. I checked on the others. All accounted for except Amy, but she's not scheduled to sleep in her own comfortable bed tonight."

Jenny chuckled. Amy was sleeping in a very small house, where her best friend lived with her mother and four other children. "Comfort is no object when you're having fun."

"Todd's door is closed, so I assume he's out cold." Mister's eyes were so compelling in this light. "I woke you up to see if you wanted to go to the diner with me."

"The diner? At this hour?" The thought sounded so deliciously decadent! And there, on neutral turf, they'd have that conversation he wanted and she probably needed. "Let me get dressed."

The Family Plan 153

Mister eyed Jenny's revealing nightgown. "Let me help. I won't forget that little cold shoulder you showed me before."

"I won't let you forget," Jenny said, getting out of bed "See?" she said, her back to him as she flicked off a thin strap and rotated her shoulder back. "Here it is again."

Mister quickly circled the bed and chased her until she flew into their bathroom and locked the door.

A few minutes later she emerged, but Mister was not in the bedroom. She threw on her warmest sweater, a woolly mohair that reached mid-thigh, buckled on a wide belt, tugged on her jeans, and softly padded down the stairs, her boots in hand.

Mister was in the kitchen, his back to Jenny. She was in a great mood for their outing—fresh, relaxed, and excited. They hadn't gone off like this during the night since she was first pregnant with Todd.

She'd have to tell Bea and ask her to keep an ear out. She'd left her bedroom door open just in case the baby cried. She approached Mister and mused aloud, "I think the baby's ready for his own room, don't you? We could put that partition up in Matthew's room—you know, have him move his video game and..." When he didn't answer, she reached out to him. There was something strange about Mister's shoulder under her hand. It was quaking.

An instantaneous and overwhelming fear gripped her heart. She gulped air and then immediately began breathing urgently and heavily. Their hour had come. Mister was going to drop the other shoe; he was going to tumble the walls down around her, tear her life from residence in her body, break her heart into a million explosive bits of shrapnel.

He turned to face her, his eyes watery and dazed. She was shaking her head no and would have said the word if she'd been able to command her voice. Mister reached out to her—the criminal imploring the victim to understand, to forgive him, to discuss his crime with him?

She pushed his hands away, and it was then that she saw

the note in Mister's fist. Had he *written* it to her? Did this man know no dignity? Where was her old Mister? Lost to another dimension? Dwelling in the outer limits?

He grabbed her shoulders and buried his face in her neck. "I couldn't keep him!" Mister whispered in a tight voice.

He couldn't keep him? Jenny's mind reeled. What was he talking about?

"I was ineffectual," Mister continued. "That day in his room, all I did was rant at him. I don't know, Jenny, he just seemed to be on a course that looked so familiar to me. I wanted him to have the chances we didn't. I wanted to spare him the pain we both have now."

For the moment Jenny ignored the implications of what Mister had said about their pain as she grasped what he was talking about. "Todd?" Jenny asked, her heart in her throat.

Mister nodded, and Jenny took the note out of his hand. She skimmed it once and then read it again, shaking her head to make sure her eyes were in straight. "They've eloped," she stated into the top of Mister's head. "They've eloped."

It wasn't really a total surprise to Jenny. Her son had been hinting at it all along. And she'd understood him. Maybe she'd been too lenient, tragically permissive, but she hadn't been able to hide her deep and intuitive understanding of her son's love for his "Pearl." And in the note Todd promised to come back by the end of the week—to finish school and to make plans for moving away to college with Peggy next year.

A tiny giggle escaped her like an ejection from her very soul. With the beginning of profound relief she giggled again, and soon her laughter grew to sobbing, encompassing a mother's emotions, a lover's relief, a woman's sensitivity.

She cried into Mister's chest when he hugged her to him. She laughed into it as he rocked them. "You mean you're not going to..." She couldn't stand the relief! "You mean you were talking about Todd?"

Mister looked at Jenny, his face sobering. He regarded her with incredulous eyes. "Your firstborn has just made one of the most important decisions of his life," he reminded her. "He's left. Why are you laughing?"

Jenny held her sides to keep them from splitting. She tried to wipe away the flood of tears that threatened to creep into her sweater. She doubled over in the strangest sobbing she'd ever known. "Because, Mister Potato-Head," she managed, "he'll be back home by the end of the week!"

Mister pulled away from her and held her at arm's length. His confused expression gradually changed to dawning understanding as Jenny's limp body sagged in his grasp. "Oh, I get it—you're hysterical! I've never known you to fall apart like this. My poor Jenny! It's a shock, isn't it?" He grabbed her and hugged her tight.

Jenny was still laughing. Part of what Mister said was absolutely true. Part of what he believed about her reaction was very intuitive and perceptive. But actually Jenny was not so much shocked by what her son had done as she was relieved by what Mister had not done.

She was brave about Todd's decision; she'd been prepared and even supportive. It went down, though very poignantly, with a full swig of the courage she'd been building all these years as a mother and wife, lover and confessor, healer and counselor.

No, she wouldn't tell Mister that she'd misunderstood his stance, his behavior, his words, when she'd first entered the kitchen. She wouldn't tell him that she'd suffered the worst shock of her life not over Todd's marriage, but over what she imagined was Mister's farewell speech. Mister was kissing her head, smoothing her hair, telling her that he was near for her. Clearly he needed to be needed by her more than he needed her courage.

Bea was suddenly in the kitchen with them. She muttered a muffled, "Oh!" and then closed the door as she exited.

Mister held on tightly to Jenny. "I'll go find him," he was telling her. "He couldn't have left so long ago. I'll bring him home again."

"No, Mister," Jenny whispered. "You don't change life by forcing decisions on people." She wiped some of her stray tears and sniffled into her husband's broad, muscular chest. "You taught us all that very lesson," she reminded him. "We've always lived by it."

She wanted him to know that his family loved and needed him, depended upon him not only for sustenance but for their very moral lives. She regretted all the times that she, the children, even Bea and Heddy, had regarded Mister as a sort of permanent fixture, a faithful, sweet, but uninteresting pet.

Jenny herself was not as guilty of this as were the others; she knew the Mister who came alive behind closed doors. The Mister who was the most exciting, warm, and sexy lover in the world. The Mister whose playfulness and gentleness were integral parts of his character. The Mister whose authority and strength came not only from being the father or the breadwinner, but from being a truly wise and masterful adult.

She remembered times when she'd let others compliment her on her youthful appearance while Mister had sat by, slightly hurt—never jealous, but always a bit left out. She recalled how he'd never discouraged men's attentions and compliments to her, but how she'd often felt secretly triumphant and bolstered. It was as though her beauty had been a good reason for Mister to revere and love her, to count himself lucky. And he'd even given her a new life by letting her work at the gallery, and by allowing Bea to live with them.

Now, at this moment, with her husband leading her out of the darkened kitchen, a love more awesome and grand than she'd ever known grew in her chest. She nuzzled closer to her husband's neck and silently vowed to change the way in which she'd allow her children, and others, to see him.

Lloyd Heath. He had so much integrity, so much power, so much wisdom, that he'd actually double-crossed himself by letting everyone else have their limelight, their recognition, their freedom.

What Karen had said in her speech about her family was true. There was probably no more fertile soil, no better

The Family Plan 157

breeding ground for individuality, than within the Heath family. But the one omission she'd made was a mention of credit. Lloyd Heath had been the quiet, rousing force behind every small and large movement any of them made. And Jenny was going to show him that she, for one, needed him. That he shouldn't go farther than the front door to be all he wanted to be.

Jenny felt his strong-muscled thighs hit her back as he lifted her and carried her up the stairs. She smelled his manly scent, felt the warmth of his chest and arms. Her body moved pliantly with his until in their room, with the door kicked closed, Mister threw her onto the bed and began to make love to her.

Jenny knew it was going to be the kind of lovemaking that stood out forever in a married woman's mind as one of those rare, excruciatingly wonderful events of her life. It was already being colored not only by all the revelations Jenny was having about her husband—that fuel for awesome and reverent desire—but by Mister's own sense of being the solace and strength in his sensitive wife's life.

Jenny wanted him to know that she really did need him, that she really was vulnerable and scared and unsure. That no matter what she'd handled in the past, the future frightened her. It didn't matter that he felt this raw surge of sexual and loving desire because he thought he was comforting her over the "loss" of their firstborn child.

What mattered was that the occasion was an opportunity for Jenny to demonstrate just how much she needed to have her husband near. To make him feel that without him, her strength would be vastly undermined. That what they'd built over the years was not only two adult individuals with all their quirks and prejudices and failings and strengths, but one unit that functioned best when attached, connected, involved.

Now, tumbling in Mister's fevered embrace and returning all his fervor with her own urgent needs, Jenny was surprised by the intensity of his passion. She was breathless over his relentless fondlings, his insistent and powerful drive.

He slipped his hand under her belt and drew her to him so that she was under his heaving body. He lavished her face with kisses that were moist and sweet and very, very persuasive. She gave him her mouth, she surrendered her chin, she let him envelop her ears with his panting, urgent breath, all the while talking to him, encouraging him, confiding her deepest sensations and emotions.

Mister unbuckled her belt and slipped two probing hands under her sweater. His fingers found her breasts and rotated the nipples with gentle, evocative motions that made Jenny's feet burn in all the spots he'd touched and rubbed before. He kept himself clothed while his hands explored her midriff, drawing it up toward his own chest and splaying his roving, electric fingers around her front and back.

He buried his head under her woolly sweater and tongued her straining body, giving her ripples of excited pleasure. She gasped for air as his warm mouth fit over a breast, and she panted, holding tightly on to his head as he nibbled the rib below the neat, tight orbs.

She tried to get his clothes off, tried to undo the buttons of his shirt and the zipper of his pants, but Mister pulled away, only to redouble his efforts.

His hands enveloped her small body, running up and down her ribcage. His lips ate at her like a hungry animal. He smoothly unzippered her jeans and dipped his hands into them so that he was cupping her buttocks and squeezing them in his palms.

Jenny felt him move away for a second and heard his own zipper coming undone. Without undressing himself or her, but with his hands and lips and legs working miracles on her heated, slightly moist flesh, Mister made love to Jenny.

With a lascivious gesture, he slinked her jeans over her buttocks, fit his palm over her pelvis, and took her then and there. The lights were out, their clothing was cunningly shifted, their muffled cries and moans came in short, ecstatic thrusts that matched, sound for touch, their escalating passion.

The Family Plan

Jenny felt the bed spinning as her husband went deeper and deeper, taking her with him into that insulated, concentrated, and wholly wondrous nest that lovers build deep in the center of the universe.

He drew her body and soul closer, and when their ecstasy came, when their burning, straining fulfillment arrived, they took their pleasure together, timing it by each other's sounds and movements, working with the infallible knowledge of each other's desires and needs. Each one called out the other's name and clung on for dear life as they spun crazily around and landed with a thump back in the world of their bedroom, where they cried gratefully and cathartically into each other's flesh.

It was only an hour later that Mister woke Jenny. Again, though now they'd undressed and were snuggled like nestled spoons in a forgotten drawer, they made love. And again, the experience, so hot and passionate and different from the first, was destined to stay with Jenny forever.

She might not have her precious Mister as long as that, but she'd have, until the end of her days, the tingling, shivering memory of what they'd done tonight.

11

WHEN JENNY AWOKE the next day, a deep red blush swept up from her tingling breasts to her neck and into her cheeks. She smiled a silly, schoolgirl grin and buried her face in her pillow. That man, she thought, giggling.

He wasn't in their room or in their bath. She found him, after she'd dressed, leaning against the counter in the kitchen and talking to Bea about the contents of the pantry shelf.

Jenny sailed in, smiling brightly, and planted happy kisses on each of the children's faces. She gave Bea a playful whack on her bottom and leaned to kiss Mister.

After last night and the intimacy they'd shared, she felt so much effervescence that she could have supplied the bottling company in Adler with enough bubbles for three truckloads of their tooth-rotting concoctions.

But Mister gave her only a terse, enigmatic smile and let her kiss the air to the side of his lips. So! He was having regrets. Seeing Mister retreat again after last night effectively burst Jenny's bubble of happiness, and throughout breakfast she and Mister kept a polite distance.

In the car she tugged sharply at her seatbelt, crossed her legs so that baby Lloyd could sit high and see out the window, and kept her gaze on the road.

"You're mad at me," Mister stated as he smoothly steered out of their driveway.

Jenny gave him a sardonic smile and said, "I understand my husband enough to know when he's hiding behind a wall of confusion."

Mister reached out to stroke her cheek with the back of his palm. "I'm sorry," he said softly, his voice a caress of love that wrapped its fingers around Jenny's heart strings. "It was unfair to have it so beautifully when I can't even think straight. Last night shouldn't have happened."

"Like hell it shouldn't have!" Jenny responded. Then she gave a sigh of frustration. "Look, Mister, I know it's against your impeccable principles to lead a girl on, but only a lobotomy could take last night away from me."

Mister laughed out loud and abruptly pulled over to the side of the road. He sat silently until she turned to meet his gaze. Those eyes—they were always her undoing. "I did mean last night," he told her, taking a curl of her blond hair in his hand and stretching it gently until he wrapped it across her nose.

Jenny swatted his hand, taking the curl in her own. Sighing, she answered, "I know you did, Mister." Then she wailed, "If only you were some nasty, macho brute! I could hate you then!"

Mister sidled over the console and took her in his arms. His breath mingled with hers before his mouth descended to whirl her away in a sensuous dance of lips and tongues. "If you're not confused by this maniac, I wish you'd illuminate him."

Jenny gave him a shove that sent him laughing to the driver's side. "It's your stupid integrity," she told him. "Why can't you just pretend you're a happily married man again?"

Mister chuckled and pulled the car onto the road again. "I am."

The Family Plan

"Pretending?"

"No, I'm very happily married to you, Jenny. I'm just a dope."

"I'll second that," she offered. "When you decide what exactly it is that you want, Mister, will you let me know?"

"Of course." They were at a stop light.

Jenny tied the baby's hat ribbons. Looking into his innocent, sparkly eyes, Jenny said, "If I thought you'd fall for it, I'd dress my six kids in rags and limp down Main Street. That might get your pity."

Mister engaged the clutch and laughed at the mental picture her words painted. In stages his laugh grew full and robust until, at the gallery driveway, he rubbed his face to sober himself. It was then that Jenny saw that his laughter was not totally happy; there was a note of sorrow in it. "You have only five," he reminded her, skirting, Jenny realized, all the other issues the image had brought to mind.

Jenny unbuckled herself and the baby and drew one long leg out of her sitting position to place it on the ground. "No," she reminded Mister, feeling that she'd done a much better job than he of adapting to the changes within their family. "Didn't you ever hear the saying, 'You're not losing a son, you're gaining another mouth to feed'?"

Mister reached to take Jenny's head in his hands, leaning her backward until his mouth savagely kissed and consumed hers. His deep gray eyes gazed long and deeply into hers. "Last night..." he began. "Well, no matter how I try to keep it straight—to not confuse the issue, to be clear and fair and honest with you—I can't help wanting to make love to you, to own you." He fit his hand around her chin and sensuously stroked it. "My God, Jenny,"—he inhaled deeply—"you've always driven me wild!"

She smiled softly and straightened up, looking needlessly to see if any of the merchants on this exclusive street had seen Lloyd's passionate display. "Maybe that's the very thing that is clear and honest, Lloyd," she said offhandedly. "Maybe you're looking for something you've already got." She left the car and took baby Lloyd into the gallery.

Mister didn't come into the shop for another ten minutes, and Jenny hoped he was out nursing a cup of coffee and mulling over what she'd said. Jenny had found Heddy already there, reviewing her packing list for the crate builders. After some business chatter about the dimensions of some of the larger structures, Heddy confided, "I got my period."

Jenny looked into her friend's eyes. "How do you feel?"

"Crampy and crabby." She showed her incisors, making Jenny howl at Heddy's gorgeous attempt at ugliness.

"C'mon, the truth."

"Relieved."

"That's very direct," she noted.

"And very true." Heddy offered the baby a sip of her milk and a bite of her English muffin. He took them calmly. "I've come to love you," Heddy began, "and Lloyd, and every one of your adorable children—"

"How about Peggy?" Jenny interrupted.

For a second, Heddy looked puzzled. Then a light dawned. "Are they planning..." She waved her hand in the air.

"By this time, I suspect she's already a Heath."

"Oh." She was silent a moment, then asked, "How do *you* feel?"

"The truth? Relieved." There were lots of reasons to feel that way, but Jenny simply said, "At least now Todd intends to go back to school." She smiled at her friend. "But I interrupted your love list," she apologized.

"Well, I love all of it, and all I've seen of your life together, and all... but, well, it's not for me, Jenny."

"Case dismissed," Jenny said, touching Heddy's slender shoulder.

"We had a big fight last night, Paul and I, after we got back from your house."

"Our house is famous for inciting riots," Jenny remarked.

Heddy laughed. "But not this kind—not between husband and wife."

"Oh no? Want to see the welts on my heart?" She playfully began unbuttoning the first button of her blouse. The baby looked up interestedly, and Jenny smiled mischie-

The Family Plan   165

vously. "Hey, kid, you're on the wagon, remember? The milk bar is closed."

"Well, then every marriage must have its problems," she reasoned.

"I'm sure," Jenny agreed. "But now what'll you do?"

Heddy walked a few paces and then retraced her footsteps. "I can't be someone I'm not just for Paul's sake, and as much as I'm unsure about why I'm doing it all, I'll be going to China with Lloyd."

"And then?" Jenny coaxed.

"Then maybe... eventually..." she sighed. "I'll have to make some kind of decision. But for now, I don't feel like making a choice. I don't want what he wants, and yet I may not want what I once did."

Jenny chuckled warmly. "Don't we all know that feeling!"

"Scary, isn't it?" Heddy asked.

"I kind of like it," Jenny mused aloud. "In a way, at least."

Mister must have come in quietly, for he suddenly appeared with a bag of rolls and coffee. *"What* do you like?" he asked his wife.

Jenny winked at Heddy. "Life's quirky nature. The chances for experience and experimentation."

"How do you two always get on these metaphysical subjects?" he marveled, laughing.

"Women aren't afraid to express themselves," Jenny explained. "We're taught early that, unlike men, we can have feelings—even be sentimental. Gives us an edge later in life; we're used to recognizing human problems—or to creatively preventing them."

Mister gave an especially comical frown that both women laughed at. "Isn't there any hope for us men?" he wailed good-naturedly.

Jenny smirked and assessed Mister. "For you," she stated laconically. "If you wake up soon enough."

"I get it," Mister hedged. "There's a secret meaning in them thar words."

"You get it!" Jenny exclaimed.

"Well, you get this: the packers will be here tomorrow, and you women are in a lot of trouble if you're not ready."

They both began a tirade against Mister. "You're the one who was so independent," Jenny accused. "You didn't even want me here."

"I was out of touch with my sentiments and emotions," he joked.

Jenny threw a coffee stirrer at him. "I'll say!"

"Get to work!"

The day went quickly and quietly, with little time for talk or speculation. That night, Jenny wanted to talk to Mister about his retreat after their extraordinary lovemaking. She wanted to get things straight with him, to finally approach him about his feelings toward their future. She certainly didn't want to be left hanging the way Paul would be during the China trip. She knew that she and Mister would have to resolve matters beforehand.

But that night Mister stayed late at the gallery while Jenny did some grocery shopping and rushed home to get dinner started so that her family wouldn't report her for child neglect.

When Mister came home, Amy was crying over a difficult math problem, which he had to help her with. After that, he took her to the clinic to have her stitches removed.

Bea and Jenny were scraping off the dinner plates when Jenny straightened up, rubbing her neck. "Stiff," she complained. "I've been hunched over all day."

"Why don't you go over to the health club?" Bea suggested.

The idea cheered Jenny. She scooted over to the refrigerator to check the evening schedule. Yes, there was a yoga class tonight, and her favorite teacher was conducting it.

"Go," Bea urged. "I'm in for the night. No panting dates or anything like that."

The class was refreshing and stimulating. Later, as Jenny stood on the steps of the health club and bade good night to the women she'd come to know, she felt entranced by the rustling of the remaining fall leaves. The clouds were rushing past the silver moon, giving Jenny the sensation that she was whisking along with them, high and fast, across the surface of the planet.

Not yet ready to call it a night, she phoned home. Joyce answered. "Is Daddy there yet?"

"No, but he called, and we told him where you were."

"Listen, I'm going to take a little ride."

"A ride?" Joyce echoed incredulously. "Why?"

"Because I'm the mother," she stated simply.

She drove into Adler and circled the small town square, which, in the light of the moon, looked ghostly and charmed. She passed the bar where she'd had her eventful rendezvous with Mister and drove beyond it to admire the fields and hills just outside of town.

On her way back, she impulsively turned into the tavern parking lot. There was a pair of lovers in the car next to hers, whispering intimately and occasionally laughing aloud. She left the chill and rustling of the moody night and entered the smoke-filled barroom, where a few couples were gyrating to the sounds of the same band that had played on her last visit.

Adjusting her electric-blue Lycra skirt that swirled over her contrasting green tights and body suit, Jenny took a place at the bar. She ordered a seltzer with a twist of lemon and sat, her legs swinging, watching the dancers. It was fun just sitting there like that, momentarily so free and untroubled.

"Claudia!" a pleasantly surprised voice boomed near her ear.

Hendrick! She remembered that she'd never given him her real name. In a way, she was happy to see him: he would be a friendly stranger, someone who could make small talk about nothing important and not even remind her that her name was Jenny Heath.

"Well, this is a real pleasure!" he said, shaking her hand as though she were an old friend. "Dance?" he asked graciously.

She nodded and said, "With reservations," as they eased

out onto the dance floor. Hendrick opened his arms, tacitly asking if she'd allow him the intimacy of the slow song that was just beginning.

Laughing, Jenny moved into his capable hold. "I have to warn you," she said, "if you want to dance and talk, okay. But nothing more. And if you're out looking for someone to bring home, then don't waste your time on me. You can go off looking before it gets any later."

"Why? Are you attached or something?"

"With manacles and steel chains," Jenny said. "I have six children."

At Hendrick's look of shock, she added, "And I might be a grandmother before the year is out; my oldest boy just eloped."

Hendrick threw his head back in merriment. "Claudia, you're a hoot!" Hoot. Jenny liked that word. Then Hendrick looked down into her face. "Did you ditch that nameless creep you met that night?"

"I'm afraid he might be ditching me," Jenny responded.

"You're better off without him," Hendrick asserted. "You'd be better off with him on the other side of the world."

"China," Jenny said.

Hendrick laughed, his bright white teeth shining in the dim light. "That would be luck!"

"Yeah, *my* luck," Jenny answered, knowing that Hendrick had no way of understanding her double entendres.

"What *was* his name?" Hendrick inquired, letting go of Jenny to smooth down his moustache.

"Mister."

"Mr. what? Mr. Clean?" He apparently thought this very funny.

Jenny thought of how Mister brushed imaginary lint from his clothes. "That's a good one," she agreed. She put her cheek on Hendrick's shoulder and felt him make an attempt to draw her closer.

Jenny immediately pulled back and gave him a stern look of reproach. Poor man—he was always getting her motherly treatment. "I told you," she stated. "I'm here just to dance and talk."

The Family Plan 169

Hendrick shook his head. "You're too much!" he said, laughing.

All of a sudden, from seemingly nowhere, Mister's voice broke in. "She's too much for *you*," he warned.

Jenny spun around, one arm still caught in Hendrick's hold. "What are you doing here?" She gasped at her husband's dark scowl.

By the ironic way he stared at her, his mouth twisted in a half smile, his eyes deadly, Jenny knew she was being asked the same question.

Hendrick sauntered around Jenny to face Mister. "Your eye healed nicely," he commented. Jenny could feel Hendrick's entire being bracing itself to deliver another punch. "Let's see if we can do as well with the other."

But before Hendrick could swing, and before Jenny could react, Mister landed a resounding wallop on Hendrick's eye. As Hendrick bent to cup it, Mister yanked on Jenny's arm and pulled her to the door.

She fought his tight fingers on her wrist and even brought them up to bite them. "You brute!" she snapped at Mister. "It wasn't his fault! He didn't believe I was—" When she realized she was almost out the door, she called into the commotion of the barroom, "I'm sorry, Hendrick!" It sounded so lame! "You're a good dancer!" she added, wincing at her own ineptitude as Mister slammed the door behind them.

He opened the door of his sports car and practically threw her inside. Swinging himself into the driver's seat and spinning gravel off the parking lot pavement, he whisked Jenny away into the moonlit night.

"I resent this!" Jenny yelled, her fists balled at her sides. "I deserved some fun after all the doubts you've been putting me through."

Mister simply looked at her and then turned his eyes back to the road.

"Well, you've been making me crazy with wondering whether you're going to decide against me," she accused.

Mister again gave her a piercing glance, and Jenny remembered their lovemaking of the other night. "You even tried to deny me that one wonderful night!" she screamed, beside herself with frustration and anger. What was she supposed to do? Simply give him all the freedom he needed while she idly stood by and watched her world come apart? Suddenly she felt drained.

"I didn't mean any harm," she defended herself. A lump formed in her throat. "I just needed to get out, see some people, talk to an impartial—" The lump got stuck, and she felt it squeezing the tears out of her eyes. She sniffled. "I feel like our house was built over a land mine," she said through her constricted throat.

Mister said nothing, and Jenny found her fingers doing a tiny, tense dance of frustration. Staring out into the crisp night, she saw that Mister was not heading home. She was about to ask where they were going, but at that point she preferred no conversation to Mister's.

They climbed the hill that led out of Adler. The trees above, with their crepe-paper leaves still attached, formed a protective tunnel that drew them deeper and deeper into the heart of the night. Jenny snuggled down into her seat, sensing, all of a sudden, that Mister intended to provide an adventure.

His well-tuned sports car turned into a private lane. Jenny twisted in her seat to read the sign, but she was too late. The curving road shaded by dark moon shadows led them to an old inn. Immediately a valet took over the car for them and pointed them toward the check-in desk.

Inn! It certainly wasn't the motel of Jenny's fantasies. She saw by the stationery on the desk that they were at the exclusive and very expensive inn run by an old established family from the area.

Jenny had too much dignity to leave her mouth hanging open the way it was now. After all, anyone seeing her would imagine that this rendezvous was a complete surprise to the little lady. Mister tugged on her arm, and she accompanied him up the grand old stairs carpeted in a maroon wool patterned with huge gray flowers. There were high benches and antique tables along the dim hallway, and when Mister opened the door to their suite, she saw three wrapped boxes

The Family Plan 171

on the bed. He politely let her step in before him, then he locked the door, pulled the sweeping drapes closed, and lit the bedside lamp.

Jenny stood, her shoulder bag under her arm, in the center of the big room. A fire was crackling in the stone fireplace.

Mister sat on the edge of the bed and removed his shoes, as if it were the most natural thing in the world to be doing. He produced a small overnight case that was on the floor beside the bed and rummaged for his robe and toothbrush. Standing up, he looked at Jenny with quizzical eyes. "Well? Aren't you going to open your boxes?"

She stared at him and then let out a laugh of surprise and puzzlement. "They're for me?" she asked.

"I'd originally planned to meet the Queen of Sheba, but when I found out she'd been dead for so long, I decided you were a good second choice," he said dryly, not cracking a smile. He turned and disappeared into the bathroom.

Jenny wiped her hands on her skirt and sat on the bed to open the first box. It was from her favorite but too-expensive-to-be-practical boutique in Piper. Inside she found the very dress she'd admired one afternoon as she, Mister, and Heddy had passed the shop on their way to lunch. It was of a pink so soft it seemed white. The chiffonlike fabric actually glistened and flowed like melted gemstones as she drew it out of its nest of bright red tissue paper.

She stood and held it up against herself, then danced around the room, ending at the fireplace. The hemline of the skirt fell in soft, uneven peaks. There was delicate beadwork along the bodice and at the cinched waist. She could tell that the neckline was going to be beautiful on her—low and wide, it would accentuate her shoulders and show just the beginning of her cleavage.

She knocked on the bathroom door, and immediately, dressed only in his tailored cotton robe, Mister appeared. His gray eyes were smoky as he looked at his wife with the dress pressed up against her body "Did you open the others?" he intoned in her favorite voice—the one that was the sexy, intimate vehicle of his desires.

She ran to the bed and opened another box. Inside was a gorgeous peignoir set of beige batiste cotton with delicate smocking of pastel silk flowers along the yoke of both the robe and the nightgown.

She looked at Mister, who was now standing behind her, his hands on her shoulders. "It's like the one you refused to buy when Matthew was born," he said softly.

"I know that," Jenny answered. "What I don't know is why you've bought me these things now."

Mister's chin pointed to the third box. It was the biggest of all, and wrapped in the same pastel foil. Jenny's fingers were trembling as she undid the bow and cluster of flowers on the box. She saw that inside there was another sea of red tissue paper. Her hands shaking, she parted the red waters but found nothing. It would be a very appropriate gift, really, this bunch of nothingness. It would be emblematic of her confusion, her empty guesses as to Mister's motives tonight. Finally her hand tapped a small box. Her eyes darted to Mister and then back toward her gift. Dare she guess it was jewelry? She fished the small leather case out of the box and held it to her cheek.

She didn't care what was in the box; she just knew that all this meant something very important to Mister. She looked up into his deep gray eyes.

"I had the girl at the shop wrap it all the same," he told her, his voice soft and gentle. "Today," he clarified. "After our little talk."

Her hands were cold as she flicked the catch on the case. Its lid sprang up to reveal a gold ring set—one ring for a man, another for a woman. They looked very old, with their intricate detailing of cherry blossoms and tiny, squiggly hieroglyphics. She cast her eyes up to catch Mister's.

"I brought them to the jewelers weeks ago," he told her. "To have them sized for us. They're from Egypt. Very rare. Very old."

Jenny threw her arms around her husband and held on to him for dear life, as though she were afloat in a big, mysterious sea. "But why?" she implored. "Why?" She pulled away slightly but still held on tightly. Her eyes were giving him all the compassion and understanding she had in her. She shook her head softly and whispered, "None of this will change how you feel, Mister."

He squeezed her to himself and rocked her until only her toes touched the lush old carpeting beneath them.

"Why?" he repeated, releasing his hold and pulling the covers off the bed. "This is for tonight," he said.

Jenny didn't want to throw cold water on their romantic adventure, but she had to ask, very gingerly, "One night in a million? And tomorrow you apply for a refund?"

Mister's straight white teeth flashed in a grin. "The first of a million more," he vowed.

Why? What had happened to answer her prayers? "Don't tell me you had a visitation from the Archangel Gabriel," she teased, feeling finally that she was getting her husband back.

Mister threw his head back in mirth. His eyes were twinkling gaily when he focused on Jenny. "You're not very far from the truth," he pronounced.

"What?" she exclaimed. She snapped her fingers in mock disappointment. "Just when I think I'm getting you back, I'll have to admit you to a loony bin!" she lamented.

Mister took her in his arms and hugged her so hard she could scarcely talk, scarcely breathe. "I'm not crazy, my precious wife. I just finally see things for what they are."

Jenny looked down into the mountainous terrain her breasts and Mister's chest made together. She was afraid to hear any more, afraid to find that this might be a temporary reprieve for her. After all, there were still the questions of Heddy, of their trip to China alone, of Mister's deep-rooted frustrations over his role in life.

He let her go and crossed the room to a small stocked bar. His walk was freer, more uninhibited than ever. If Jenny didn't know better, she'd believe he was slightly inebriated. He talked as he worked, opening a bottle of champagne and unscrewing the cap on a bottle of seltzer. "I hope you'll join me in a toast before you resort to your old favorite—

seltzer," he suggested. She nodded from across the room, waiting for some illumination of this behavior and attitude.

"You know, Jenny," Mister—the old Mister—said enthusiastically. "I've been a pain in the donkey's seat." She nodded agreement. "But I've been thinking—thinking very hard since that day I first admitted that I was having a crisis of my own."

He gave her a crystal champagne glass and looked her in the eyes.

"What are we celebrating?" she asked.

"The occasion of our son's marriage," he replied.

Jenny blinked but didn't dare ask what had precipitated Mister's change of heart. She knew how fragile his approval might be. She sipped with Mister and waited, afraid to ask anything.

He continued as he fluffed up her new dress and held it against her. "I talked to him and Peggy earlier, you know."

Jenny's heart skipped two beats and then painfully took up a tirade that would have made her the pride of Brazilian folk drummers.

"He talked to me as though I were—I don't know," Mister continued, "a stranger, or something. He wanted to see you, of course, but after a while we started talking like we used to, and I heard his happiness, his conviction that he was right, his maturity, his vulnerability, his—" Mister stopped talking to gaze into Jenny's eyes, which, she knew, were probably wide and unbelieving. "Didn't you guess it, my dear, lovely Guinevere? Didn't you know why I reacted so badly to his plans?"

"You wanted him to have what you never had?" she ventured truthfully.

She hadn't heard Mister laugh as exuberantly and freely in what seemed like a lifetime. He cupped her chin and gazed so unabashedly and so lovingly into her eyes that Jenny felt her cheeks blushing. "You're so sweet!" he exclaimed. "And so silly for such an accomplished woman— which, by the way, brings me to another realization this fool head of mine was ignoring. For years—really, Jenny, for years—I should have been praising you, letting you know how much you meant to me and the kids. I guess after not hearing it enough, you sort of began to believe that you were lacking something, and that gave you that terrible restlessness. The funny thing is that all the while you'd been picking up some very useful skills. They came out while you worked at the gallery."

Jenny was nodding yes, she was shaking her head no, she was trying to keep pace with Mister's reasoning. He laughed at what must have been her comical expression and hugged her again, this time taking a deep, liberating breath when he let go.

"You remember that day in Todd's room?"

Did she ever! It had been one of the most frustrating and painful moments of her relationship with her family, and it had set off a terrible reaction in Mister. She nodded, took another sip, and sat down, the beautiful dress draped across her exercise clothes.

"Don't you see?" Mister urged. "He was so sure, so cock-sure, that it triggered a memory in me—the memory of how I felt when I first knew I just had to have you for my own. By talking to him, by arguing and fighting with him, I saw that I was fighting with myself."

He stood before Jenny, gesticulating in his refined, expressive way. "I tell you," he said, "it's very sobering to be giving advice to someone who is the exact image of yourself when you were experiencing just what he's experiencing now!"

Jenny's head was still trying to keep pace with the ideas that Mister seemed to find so enlightening. Her eyes were fixed on her husband as she tried, with all her heart and soul, to follow him.

"I was feeling empathetic after a while," he told her. "And in feeling that way, I got angrier and angrier. Here was my son, my very double, presenting all the reasons why he should stay with his beloved, while I knew, I *knew* deep inside, that I felt the same exact way about my own wife."

He took Jenny by the hands and made her stand up. The dress fell from her lap. Scooping it up, he tossed it onto the bed and muttered, "Mustn't dirty it before Saturday."

Jenny thought she was beginning to get a clearer picture of what Mister was saying. In being so close to the emotions Todd had been describing, Mister had been threatened with feeling precisely what he didn't want to feel for Jenny. He wanted, perhaps, what she'd often wished for—a mean ogre for a mate, someone from whom it would be easy to separate. Someone for whom there was no love, no "cornstarch," no fidelity. Feeling that the grass was greener elsewhere, that one wanted to be out on one's own while there was so much substance right at home, was antithetical. Jenny had become, in essence, the enemy to Mister's imagined desires, needs, and wants. But Saturday?

She eyed him quizzically.

"They'll be home tomorrow. That's why I had to find you tonight." He put his hand to his forehead. "That man in the bar!" he exclaimed.

Jenny tittered at the memory of Hendrick. "I'll have to make it up to him somehow, poor confused thing."

"Invite him to the party."

"Party?"

"Saturday. I told Peggy that I was sure you'd want to have an official celebration with friends and relatives—a way of easing her into our lives." He stopped to draw Jenny closer to the fire.

In the glow of the flames Mister looked so handsome, so devilishly sexy, so irresistible to the woman who had loved him since she first understood the word, and who had stood by him throughout this terrible storm.

"That's where the dress comes in," he explained. "She could have gotten one for us in white, but really..." His eyes were bright with sexy insinuation. Jenny felt her thighs weakening and turning to molten flesh. "White wouldn't be quite appropriate. Pink—that soft, whispery pink—was better for you. It's a slight shade off white, perfect for the blemished bride."

Jenny put her champagne glass onto the mantel. Maybe

The Family Plan

it *was* getting to her. "What?" she asked, feeling more than a little confused.

"The rings," Mister said sensibly. "I was saving them for our twentieth, but this occasion seems so much more appropriate." At his wife's befuddlement, Mister clarified, "To renew our vows. Our vows, Jenny. Of love,"—he drew her closer still, and she could feel his hard bough of desire between them—"and fidelity." His lips descended to hers, and Jenny could taste the sweet champagne on his breath before their moist lips met to melt deliciously and sensuously together. "We'll renew our vows when Todd and Peggy renew theirs."

"Oh!" The light was dawning. "Oh!" she breathed huskily into his mouth as she pressed herself closer to him and rubbed her hips, like a straining animal, against his hard and muscular form.

Mister picked her up and placed her on the rug before the fire. He darted to get the blanket off the bed and then lay himself on top of her, the cover thrown around them like a shroud protecting deep secrets.

They kissed before the fire like that, heating the air under the blanket and feeling each other's bodies with practiced, familiar, and loving fingers. This time it was Mister who was naked first, and Jenny took full advantage of the situation, lavishing attention on him.

"But all the other things, Lloyd?" Jenny asked softly wanting answers but not wanting to break the mood.

"China?" he asked her before his tongue teased the roof of her mouth. "Come, too," he said. "We have Bea now, and Peggy will be around, and God knows our kids don't need us!"

"They need us," Jenny corrected, "but not like before." She held the back of Mister's head and took one sweet kiss before she dropped the bomb of her next question. Ironically, it came out in one word, just as it had from Mister's mouth when it had meant as much. "Heddy?" she whispered.

But Mister didn't move a muscle except to kiss his wife more deeply.

"You knew it all along," he said. "You've been hinting

at it, and I've been resisting because I felt I had something at stake."

Jenny took a gulp of air and laughed loudly. A frozen chunk of understanding was freed in the ocean of her mind. Mister had both recognized and ignored his reasons for being attracted to Heddy. No wonder he'd given Jenny such mixed messages! "I was wondering when you were going to see that you were projecting onto her, that you had a kind of fascination for the way she'd been able to do what you hadn't."

"She reminded me of something I might have been if not for the choices I'd made," Mister added. Then he brought his sexy mouth to within an inch of his wife's and gave her a big smile that lit his gray, Lloyd eyes. "I must have looked very foolish imagining I could have what an eighteen-year-old boy and a thirty-something-year-old woman could."

"But you do have those things!" Jenny protested.

"Oh," Mister corrected, "I don't mean I don't have the love of my life, or a really satisfying business. I mean it was stupid to compare myself to them when what I have—what we have together—is really, well, for lack of a better word..."—his eyes smiled as he raised his eyebrows, "better." He gave her a sudden kiss that tore the breath from her lungs and instantly stoked the fire he'd already ignited.

Jenny pulled her mouth away. There was still so much talking to do, and she couldn't let her passion blur it. "Then you're not in love with her?" she asked. "Even a little bit?"

Mister bit her nose. "I told you that from the beginning. Don't you see? I was her cheering section because I was defending things I felt I needed."

"But now?" Jenny persisted even as Mister's hands traced the lines of her face and one fingertip dipped into her mouth. "Don't you still need that freedom you spoke of, that free-wheeling life?"

Mister snuggled closer to her and leaned his cheek on hers. He whispered, "What should I do? Trapise around the world alone and collect ashtrays from hotels? No, I finally see what you've been trying to tell me. We have a lot of freedom coming up. I've waited this long, I can hold out some more."

He winked before going on. "Besides, you and baby Lloyd are doing a great job of keeping the place in shape. I think I'll tackle a few projects I'd felt too overloaded to do. And you two can stay home selling chests of drawers and tapestries."

Jenny playfully punched Mister in his solid side. "So? You plan to go ahead and do whatever you want anyway?" she exclaimed, her eyebrows high.

Mister's strong naked shoulders lifted in a shrug as he looked at his wife. "Somewhat," he answered. "And eventually you and I can get away for longer and longer periods. Wouldn't you be happy usurping the business out from under me?" he teased.

"You have a point there," she agreed, laughing and wrapping her leotard-clad legs around his naked buttocks.

"It's funny," he mused. "The very things we set up years ago, and that recently seemed like such shackles instead of joys, are now going to give us the freedom to explore. Our oldest son's wife wants to stay home and take care of our kids—"

"And their own, eventually, no doubt," Jenny put in.

"Our big house that required a helping hand has now adopted Bea. Our teenagers are eager to prove themselves capable and mature, and our little ones are asserting their individuality."

"Even baby Lloyd," Jenny said.

Mister nodded and smiled. "We *did* make the right choices." He raised his head in a cocky swagger. "And we did a great job."

"Bea says, 'The fruit doesn't fall far from the tree.'"

"Now, there's one that makes sense! You ought to get her a book of proverbs."

"I already bought her an empty book to write her own in," Jenny countered.

Mister smiled and slid his hands along Jenny's hitched-up skirt. It encountered the snug leotard. He muttered a minor expletive and then began stroking Jenny's thighs through the fabric that was like a second skin anyway. "Every time you complained about not having excitement, my dear girl," he began, "some emergency needed your attention. Every time you thought yourself unfit for something, you challenged it and won."

Jenny could tell it was getting harder for Mister to concentrate on making a point. She unclasped her skirt and slipped it off. Mister groaned in appreciation. His expert hand slid into the shoulder of her leotard and slipped it languorously down her arm. His tongue followed the movements of his hand, kissing and licking his wife until she cried out in sweet agony. She wriggled her other shoulder out and worked the leotard down.

She couldn't believe the relief and excitement Mister's peace with himself gave her. She clasped his head. "Am I really coming to China with you and Heddy?"

Mister let out a tiny sound of frustration as his concentration was broken. "Just us," he whispered, his mouth not letting go of her skin.

He looked so gorgeous in the firelight. His skin reflected the orange glow; his hair was streaked with bright highlights that shimmered and danced across his head. Love swelled anew in Jenny's chest.

"What about a translator?" she teased.

Mister groaned in frustration. "After your coup with the Ming vases, I doubt we'll need anyone other than the official guide."

Jenny smiled at the compliment but persisted, "Why not Heddy? Because of Paul?"

Mister nodded. "Let's leave them here to battle it out. They need that, don't you think?"

Jenny chuckled. "You matchmaker!" Then she asked, "Do you think they'll be happy?"

Mister's crow's-feet wrinkled sexily at the corners of his loving eyes. "Not as much as we are," he said softly. "But, as Bea would undoubtedly remind them, no use traveling when there's fighting to be done."

They laughed together at the mental image of their friend and housekeeper dispensing the advice.

"Now will you please stop talking and put that gorgeous mouth of yours to some gainful use?" Mister teased.

"First I have to call the kids."

"Bea has the number here."

"Oh."

"Say that again."

"What?"

"Oh."

"Oh," Jenny repeated, and Mister took advantage of her lips' shape to kiss her, rotating and pressing their soft mouths together until they fused into one straining entity.

Breathlessly, Jenny reminded him, "We'd better stop this; kissing gives you babies!"

Her husband groaned sexily. "I'm no fool," he whispered, fumbling under the blanket for his discarded robe. He winked at her mischievously as he showed her what had been in his pocket.

"Six kids," Jenny teased. "We're fast learners!"

Mister wrapped his arms tightly under her and turned her so that she was on top of him. He smiled and ran both hands into her curls, then he slid them onto her bare shoulders, clearly reveling in the warmth and feel of her skin. She helped him take off the skin-tight leotard and tights, and then leaned down onto his chest, inhaling as she thrilled at the feel of fire-warmed skin on skin.

"Fast learners," Mister echoed into her desirous mouth. "And partners, too."

"'Til the end," Jenny whispered, her heart almost bursting, like a bird about to sing.

"A new beginning," Mister corrected. "Now, please, Jenny, be quiet."

"Don't you want to hear about my fantasy lover?" she teased, choking softly on the laugh of relief and mischief that welled up in her.

Mister stopped his hands and stared at her. "Does he look like me?" he asked suspiciously.

"Always did," Jenny chuckled, pretending to be resigned.

"Oh." He appeared to consider that. Then his eyes darted askance—into his thoughts, into his memory, Jenny guessed. He suddenly grabbed her and rotated their loving bodies until she was beneath him. "Some other time," he said apologetically. "Right now my thoughts aren't going any farther than the length and breadth of my own wife's love."

NEW FROM THE PUBLISHERS OF *SECOND CHANCE AT LOVE!*

To Have and to Hold

___ **THE TESTIMONY #1** by Robin James (06928-0)
After six dark months apart, dynamic Jesse Ludan is a coming home to his vibrant wife Christine. They are united by shared thoughts and feelings, but sometimes they seem like strangers as they struggle to reaffirm their love.

___ **A TASTE OF HEAVEN #2** by Jennifer Rose (06929-9)
Dena and Richard Klein share a life of wedded bliss...until Dena launches her own restaurant. She goes from walking on air to walking on eggs—until she and Richard get their marriage cooking again.

___ **TREAD SOFTLY #3** by Ann Cristy (06930-2)
Cady Densmore's love for her husband Rafe doesn't dim during the dangerous surgery that restores his health, or during the long campaign to reelect him to the Senate. But misunderstandings threaten the very foundation of their marriage.

___ **THEY SAID IT WOULDN'T LAST #4** by Elaine Tucker (06931-0)
When Glory Mathers, a successful author, married Wade Wilson, an out-of-work actor, all the gossips shook their heads. Now, ten years later, Wade is a famous film star and Glory feels eclipsed...

___ **GILDED SPRING #5** by Jenny Bates (06932-9)
Kate yearns to have Adam's child, the ultimate expression of their abiding love. But impending parenthood unleashes fears and uncertainties that threaten to unravel the delicate fabric of their marriage.

___ **LEGAL AND TENDER #6** by Candice Adams (06933-7)
When Linny becomes her lawyer husband's legal secretary, she's sure that being at Wes's side by day...and in his arms at night...can only improve their marriage. But misunderstandings arise...

___ **THE FAMILY PLAN #7** by Nuria Wood (06934-5)
Jenny fears domesticity may be dulling her marriage, but her struggles to expand her horizons—and reawaken her husband's desire—provoke family confusion and comic catastrophe.

All Titles are $1.95

Available at your local bookstore or return this form to:

SECOND CHANCE AT LOVE
Book Mailing Service
P.O. Box 690, Rockville Centre, NY 11571

Please send me the titles checked above. I enclose _____ Include 75¢ for postage and handling if one book is ordered; 25¢ per book for two or more not to exceed $1.75. California, Illinois, New York and Tennessee residents please add sales tax.

NAME_____

ADDRESS_____

CITY_____ STATE/ZIP_____

(allow six weeks for delivery)   THTH #67

DON'T MISS THESE TITLES IN THE SECOND CHANCE AT LOVE SERIES

STRANGER IN PARADISE #154
by Laurel Blake

Nicole Starr managed the Seawinds boutique very well without Grant Sutton's expert advice. Now he is determined to change much more than just her business practices...

KISSED BY MAGIC #155
by Kay Robbins

In a whimsical conspiracy, company president Rebel Sinclair temporarily assigns her power to Donovan, her male secretary. Is his sudden—and outrageous—seduction really to win her heart...or her chain of hotels?

LOVESTRUCK #156
by Margot Leslie

He's a tall, blond stranger who calls her Lady Luck. She's a promising playwright revising her script for Broadway. From the first, their onstage antagonism sparks offstage passion...

DEEP IN THE HEART #157
by Lynn Lawrence

Carrie Chandler arrives in rugged west Texas in search of a rare antique locomotive. But in Bat Bartholomew's powerful embrace she finds something of far greater value...

SEASON OF MARRIAGE #158
by Diane Crawford

Julie Logan's coveted assignment to interview reclusive vintner Jonathan Brook precipitates a professional crisis... and personal heartache...when she falls in love—then learns the secret behind his initial hostility...

THE LOVING TOUCH #159
by Aimée Duvall

Cassie's new boss at the Albuquerque City Zoo sends her senses reeling! Inadvertently she sets off one comical mishap after another...until Paul finally holds her close...

WATCH FOR 6 NEW TITLES EVERY MONTH!

Second Chance at Love

- ___ 06540-4 **FROM THE TORRID PAST #49** Ann Cristy
- ___ 06544-7 **RECKLESS LONGING #50** Daisy Logan
- ___ 05851-3 **LOVE'S MASQUERADE #51** Lillian Marsh
- ___ 06148-4 **THE STEELE HEART #52** Jocelyn Day
- ___ 06422-X **UNTAMED DESIRE #53** Beth Brookes
- ___ 06651-6 **VENUS RISING #54** Michelle Roland
- ___ 06595-1 **SWEET VICTORY #55** Jena Hunt
- ___ 06575-7 **TOO NEAR THE SUN #56** Aimée Duvall
- ___ 05625-1 **MOURNING BRIDE #57** Lucia Curzon
- ___ 06411-4 **THE GOLDEN TOUCH #58** Robin James
- ___ 06596-X **EMBRACED BY DESTINY #59** Simone Hadary
- ___ 06660-5 **TORN ASUNDER #60** Ann Cristy
- ___ 06573-0 **MIRAGE #61** Margie Michaels
- ___ 06650-8 **ON WINGS OF MAGIC #62** Susanna Collins
- ___ 05816-5 **DOUBLE DECEPTION #63** Amanda Troy
- ___ 06675-3 **APOLLO'S DREAM #64** Claire Evans
- ___ 06689-3 **SWEETER THAN WINE #78** Jena Hunt
- ___ 06690-7 **SAVAGE EDEN #79** Diane Crawford
- ___ 06692-3 **THE WAYWARD WIDOW #81** Anne Mayfield
- ___ 06693-1 **TARNISHED RAINBOW #82** Jocelyn Day
- ___ 06694-X **STARLIT SEDUCTION #83** Anne Reed
- ___ 06695-8 **LOVER IN BLUE #84** Aimée Duvall
- ___ 06696-6 **THE FAMILIAR TOUCH #85** Lynn Lawrence
- ___ 06697-4 **TWILIGHT EMBRACE #86** Jennifer Rose
- ___ 06698-2 **QUEEN OF HEARTS #87** Lucia Curzon
- ___ 06851-9 **A MAN'S PERSUASION #89** Katherine Granger
- ___ 06852-7 **FORBIDDEN RAPTURE #90** Kate Nevins
- ___ 06853-5 **THIS WILD HEART #91** Margarett McKean
- ___ 06854-3 **SPLENDID SAVAGE #92** Zandra Colt
- ___ 06855-1 **THE EARL'S FANCY #93** Charlotte Hines
- ___ 06858-6 **BREATHLESS DAWN #94** Susanna Collins
- ___ 06859-4 **SWEET SURRENDER #95** Diana Mars
- ___ 06860-8 **GUARDED MOMENTS #96** Lynn Fairfax
- ___ 06861-6 **ECSTASY RECLAIMED #97** Brandy LaRue
- ___ 06862-4 **THE WIND'S EMBRACE #98** Melinda Harris
- ___ 06863-2 **THE FORGOTTEN BRIDE #99** Lillian Marsh
- ___ 06864-0 **A PROMISE TO CHERISH #100** LaVyrle Spencer
- ___ 06866-7 **BELOVED STRANGER #102** Michelle Roland
- ___ 06867-5 **ENTHRALLED #103** Ann Cristy
- ___ 06869-1 **DEFIANT MISTRESS #105** Anne Devon
- ___ 06870-5 **RELENTLESS DESIRE #106** Sandra Brown
- ___ 06871-3 **SCENES FROM THE HEART #107** Marie Charles
- ___ 06872-1 **SPRING FEVER #108** Simone Hadary
- ___ 06873-X **IN THE ARMS OF A STRANGER #109** Deborah Joyce
- ___ 06874-8 **TAKEN BY STORM #110** Kay Robbins
- ___ 06899-3 **THE ARDENT PROTECTOR #111** Amanda Kent

All of the above titles are $1.75 per copy

SK-41a

___07200-1 **A LASTING TREASURE #112** Cally Hughes $1.95
___07203-6 **COME WINTER'S END #115** Claire Evans $1.95
___07212-5 **SONG FOR A LIFETIME #124** Mary Haskell $1.95
___07213-3 **HIDDEN DREAMS #125** Johanna Phillips $1.95
___07214-1 **LONGING UNVEILED #126** Meredith Kingston $1.95
___07215-X **JADE TIDE #127** Jena Hunt $1.95
___07216-8 **THE MARRYING KIND #128** Jocelyn Day $1.95
___07217-6 **CONQUERING EMBRACE #129** Ariel Tierney $1.95
___07218-4 **ELUSIVE DAWN #130** Kay Robbins $1.95
___07219-2 **ON WINGS OF PASSION #131** Beth Brookes $1.95
___07220-6 **WITH NO REGRETS #132** Nuria Wood $1.95
___07221-4 **CHERISHED MOMENTS #133** Sarah Ashley $1.95
___07222-2 **PARISIAN NIGHTS #134** Susanna Collins $1.95
___07233-0 **GOLDEN ILLUSIONS #135** Sarah Crewe $1.95
___07224-9 **ENTWINED DESTINIES #136** Rachel Wayne $1.95
___07225-7 **TEMPTATION'S KISS #137** Sandra Brown $1.95
___07226-5 **SOUTHERN PLEASURES #138** Daisy Logan $1.95
___07227-3 **FORBIDDEN MELODY #139** Nicola Andrews $1.95
___07228-1 **INNOCENT SEDUCTION #140** Cally Hughes $1.95
___07229-X **SEASON OF DESIRE #141** Jan Mathews $1.95
___07230-3 **HEARTS DIVIDED #142** Francine Rivers $1.95
___07231-1 **A SPLENDID OBSESSION #143** Francesca Sinclaire $1.95
___07232-X **REACH FOR TOMORROW #144** Mary Haskell $1.95
___07233-8 **CLAIMED BY RAPTURE #145** Marie Charles $1.95
___07234-6 **A TASTE FOR LOVING #146** Frances Davies $1.95
___07235-4 **PROUD POSSESSION #147** Jena Hunt $1.95
___07236-2 **SILKEN TREMORS #148** Sybil LeGrand $1.95
___07237-0 **A DARING PROPOSITION #149** Jeanne Grant $1.95
___07238-9 **ISLAND FIRES #150** Jocelyn Day $1.95
___07239-7 **MOONLIGHT ON THE BAY #151** Maggie Peck $1.95
___07240-0 **ONCE MORE WITH FEELING #152** Melinda Harris $1.95
___07241-9 **INTIMATE SCOUNDRELS #153** Cathy Thacker $1.95
___07242-7 **STRANGER IN PARADISE #154** Laurel Blake $1.95
___07243-5 **KISSED BY MAGIC #155** Kay Robbins $1.95
___07244-3 **LOVESTRUCK #156** Margot Leslie $1.95
___07245-1 **DEEP IN THE HEART #157** Lynn Lawrence $1.95
___07246-X **SEASON OF MARRIAGE #158** Diane Crawford $1.95
___07247-8 **THE LOVING TOUCH #159** Aimée Duvall $1.95

Available at your local bookstore or return this form to:

SECOND CHANCE AT LOVE
Book Mailing Service
P.O. Box 690, Rockville Centre, NY 11571

Please send me the titles checked above. I enclose _____. Include 75¢ for postage and handling if one book is ordered; 25¢ per book for two or more not to exceed $1.75. California, Illinois, New York and Tennessee residents please add sales tax.

NAME _____

ADDRESS _____

CITY _____ STATE/ZIP _____

(allow six weeks for delivery)   SK-41b